GREEN CARD BLUES

Sha

THE O'BRIEN PRESS
DUBLIN

First published 1994 by The O'Brien Press Ltd., 20 Victoria Road, Rathgar, Dublin 6, Ireland.

10 9 8 7 6 5 4 3 2 1

British Library Cataloguing-in-publication Data
Healy, Shay
Green Card Blues
I.Title
823.914 [F]

ISBN 0-86278-386-0

Typesetting, editing, layout: The O'Brien Press Ltd.
Cover illustration: Fionán Healy
Cover design: Neasa Ní Chianáin
Cover separations: Lithoset Ltd., Dublin
Printing: Cox & Wyman Ltd., Reading

CHAPTER ONE

Danny Toner could scarcely believe his eyes when he saw the pair of brogues sitting invitingly on the lid of a trashcan. He picked them up and scrutinised them. The soles and heels were a bit worn, but the sturdy brown uppers were hardly creased. The laces showed no trace of overuse either, but, best of all, etched into the leather of the insteps, was size 42 – Danny's size.

He looked down at the black canvas basketball boots he was wearing. For two weeks Danny had been traipsing around the streets of New York, dropping demos of his songs into record companies and music publishers, walking block after block in boots that had thin flat soles and no heels.

He held the brogues up to the light of the hard March sun, turning them this way and that, looking for some flaw that would allow him to reject them. But they were almost unblemished, a shining miracle from heaven, incandescent in his hand.

Danny glanced up and down the busy New York street to see if anyone was watching. Don't be an eejit, he told himself. Take them. So what if somebody sees? Nobody knows who you are. And even if they did, so fucking what?

He removed his boots, fumbling and cursing to himself as he tugged the laces through the eyeholes. 'Holy Jaysus,' he muttered. 'If my mother could see me now, she'd turn in her grave.'

He dumped his boots in the trashcan, slipped on the brogues and laced them up. They looked all wrong with his canvas jeans and leather jacket but, just standing in them, he could already feel the comfort of the cushioned sole.

Danny continued up Ninth Street, a half-smile of satisfaction playing on his lips. Wearing another man's shoes was a triumph over his middle-class upbringing, an act of assertion about himself. The Big Apple was about survival and at last Danny felt like he had clicked into a New York state of mind.

In his mind a tune was playing, 'If I can make it here I'll make it anywhere ...'

Danny came back up into the sunlight from the bowels of Twenty-eighth Street subway station and walked two blocks to Second Avenue. He turned the corner and there it was, My Wild Irish Rose, Bar and Restaurant.

His heart sank a little. From the outside the place looked drab and unpromising and the paintwork was starting to peel on the windows and doors.

Danny gripped his guitar firmly and pushed the door open. After the harsh glare of the sunlight, it took his eyes a few seconds to adjust to the gloom. Two solitary drinkers sipped beer at the bar which ran the length of the right-hand side of the room.

In the window alcove at one end of the bar a jukebox stood bright and silent, but, in the background, Danny could hear someone playing Paddy Reilly singing 'The Fields of Athenry'. A series of high tables and stools separated the bar from the raised performance area, which faced clusters of dark wood tables and bentwood chairs. In the other window alcove Danny noticed the microphone stand and amplifier. Through the window he could see the traffic passing on Second Avenue. At least everyone had a view of the stage. He would have a sporting chance of getting through to the audience.

The canopy over the bar and the walls were decorated with posters advertising beer and shamrocks. St Patrick's Day was only three days away and Danny had already noticed leprechauns and shamrocks popping up in the bars, restaurants and shop windows all over New York.

Still, he'd got a gig a week singing here, why worry

about the decor or the leprechauns? It was New York, he was singing and, better still, he was getting paid.

Jack Killoran flashed a quick glance around the bar to make sure no one was watching him. He poured himself a generous shot of whiskey and, turning his back on the bar, threw back the whiskey in one gulp. He grimaced as the liquor burnt its way down his throat and then he turned quickly round again, shoved the glass under the tap in the sink and rinsed it with cold water. He held it up to the light, hawed on it with his whiskey breath, wiped it clean with his dishcloth and replaced it face down on a glass shelf behind him.

He looked up and saw Danny coming towards him. Jack was well pleased. The first half of Danny's gig had gone down well. He had been better than Jack had hoped. Paddy Ryan, the owner, was always landing him with talentless friends of friends in need of a favour, but Danny could sing and he knew how to keep the punters amused – and drinking. Everyone who had come in tonight had stayed for at least two sets.

Jack had been worried about filling the St Patrick's Day slot, but now he was happy that Danny would be perfect. And what's more Danny seemed a decent guy.

'Danny, how's about you?' There was no mistaking the hard Belfast inflection coming through Jack's New York accent. 'Will you have a beer?'

'Okay,' said Danny, sitting on a stool and watching Jack pour the drink. He guessed Jack to be in his forties, with his jowls well on the way to becoming rolls of fat. The guy wasn't exactly the type Danny would hang out with back home in Dublin, but he'd given Danny a friendly welcome and that was worth a lot in this city.

Jack handed him the glass. 'So how d'you think it's going?'

'I think it's going all right. I really appreciate the gig, Jack.' Danny hesitated for a moment. 'By the way, you've probably noticed I don't do any political stuff. Is that okay with you?'

'Better than all right – a bloody relief,' answered Jack.

Danny was glad. He had said a fervent prayer that My Wild Irish Rose wouldn't turn out to be another bucket-of-blood-die-for-Ireland, New York hell-hole. 'Is this the normal crowd?'

Jack ran an eye over his customers. 'They're a bit younger on a Saturday night. A bit more hip.'

'You mean more kind of East Village types?'

'Not quite as depressing as that,' Jack said, laughing. 'Of course, you're living down there, aren't you?'

'Yeah. A pal of mine has a share in a three-bedroom apartment down on East Sixth Street,' Danny answered. 'So I'm dossing there for as long as he's out of town.'

'How are you finding it?'

'Full of groovies,' answered Danny. 'And all dressed in black. It's like being at a permanent funeral.' He paused.

'In spite of all that, I like it really. But they could do with giving the streets a few names.'

'What d'you mean?'

'Avenue A? Avenue B? Give me a break! Some gobshite short on imagination got that gig.'

'Alphabet City – that's what they call it down there.'

'Well, it's nice to know I have such a swanky address. Home of junkies, dealers, artists and tarts.' Danny picked up his glass and stood up. 'So how long do you want me to do for the last round-up?'

'Twenty minutes, half an hour. You can play it by ear.'

Danny nodded. 'Always do,' he said. He picked up his glass and loped back on stage.

The bar door swung open. A woman dressed in a leather biker's jacket and shiny leggings flounced in. She took a slow look around, smiled up at Danny and walked to the end of the bar where she sat facing the stage.

She stuck out like a sore thumb among the regulars. She had a round pretty face, with cropped black hair and a kiss curl that fell down on to her forehead. Bright red lipstick gave her a pouty look and she was rolling a wad of chewing gum around in her mouth.

She called to Jack down the bar. 'Gimme a Rollin' Rock and whatever the singer's having,' she said.

'Are you a friend of Danny's?'

'D'you have to be to buy him a drink?' she asked spikily.

Jack shrugged. He was used to New York rudeness. He flicked the cap off her beer and started to pour it into a glass. She waved the glass aside and tipped the bottle to her lips. He pulled the whiskey bottle from the tray in front of him and waved it gently until he caught Danny's eye and signalled her offer of a drink.

Danny raised his glass and flashed his benefactress a smile. She blew him a kiss in reply. She was probably in her late twenties, like himself, Danny calculated. And definitely the most interesting-looking customer who had come in all evening.

He sneaked a look at the watch which he always wore on the underside of his wrist when he was gigging. The audience response hadn't been too bad for a first night. There was still a handful of stragglers sitting at the tables in front of the stage, but most of them were now talking to one another.

Apart from the newcomer, there were only two other punters at the bar and Danny could see that they were getting ready to leave.

Good man, Jack, thought Danny. There's the signal to wrap it up for tonight. I'll just say goodnight to the punters and see what this looker has to say for herself.

He tapped the mike for attention. 'Well, folks, that's it from me, Danny Toner, after another exciting night of music and drama here at My Wild Irish Rose. I'll be here every Tuesday and also on good old St Paddy's Day when everyone has licence to behave like a complete eejit. So until then, safe home and may you be in heaven an hour before the devil knows you're dead.'

Danny unhooked the strap on his guitar and laid the instrument against the amplifier. He slid the dimmer knob on the spotlight down until the stage was in darkness and walked across to the bar where the girl sat.

She looked up as he approached.

'Thanks for the drink,' he said, picking up the strange cocktail Jack had made him.

'My pleasure,' she said in what sounded like an exaggerated New York accent. 'Hey, that was pretty, what you said there.' Danny looked at her quizzically.

'Y'know, about being in heaven before the devil?'

'Oh yeah.' Danny grinned. 'That's what they call "Blarney".'

'Blarney? Yeah. I thought you were pretty good anyway. I never heard most of them songs before, but I like your singing.'

'Well, thank you, ma'am.' Danny smiled. 'May I buy you a drink in return?'

'Sure,' she purred. 'I'll have a Rollin' Rock.'

Danny picked up her bottle of beer from the counter and held it up until he caught Jack's eye. Jack nodded.

'What's that you're drinking?' she asked. 'It looks like a soda.'

'It's a Flag. I spent half an hour earlier teaching Jack, the barman, how to perfect it. It's Creme de Menthe, whiskey and cream, the green, white and gold of the Irish flag.'

'That's cute.'

'Very cute,' said Danny, taking a swig. 'I invented it myself. People keep asking me to sing songs about dying for Ireland and I keep telling them I'd rather drink for Ireland instead.'

'Oh yeah,' she said lamely.

He could see she was puzzled. 'Do you know anything at all about Ireland?'

'Sure I do,' she said defensively. 'I'm Irish.'

'You're Irish?'

'Well, my great grandfather was Irish and I went to Catholic school and I know that the British are beating the shit out of the Catholics all the time.'

'Don't get annoyed,' Danny said, 'but it's not quite as straightforward as that.'

'Oh yeah!' she snarled, standing up suddenly. 'So how straightforward is it then?'

'Hold everything,' Danny said. 'We're getting off to a very bad start here. Let's go from the top again. My name is Danny Toner and I come from Dublin, Ireland. Thank you for buying me a drink. I never discuss politics with people I don't know and I'm very pleased to meet you.'

He stretched out his hand and she looked at him for a moment. Then the full red mouth softened into a crooked grin. 'Likewise,' she said.

'You still haven't told me your name.'

'Jazz, Jazz Ma*hony*,' she said.

'Well, that's definitely Irish,' Danny said with a grin.

'Except we pronounce it differently. We say *Mah*ony.'

'Oh yeah,' she said. '*Mah*ony. That's kinda cute.'

'D'you mind if I sit down?' Danny asked, pulling a bar stool up close to her.

She shrugged. 'It's a free country – except nothing is free, right?'

'Right.' Danny felt a smile sneaking on to the corners of his mouth. This sounded like dialogue from a sitcom. 'Jazz, d'you mind if I ask you what you do for a living?'

She looked up slowly from her bottle of beer until she was staring straight into Danny's face.

'I'm a cop.'

'Holy shit!' Danny spluttered a mouthful of drink on to the back of his hand.

'That's what they all say.'

CHAPTER TWO

The last two customers bade Jack goodnight as they walked out the door.

'G'night,' Jack called after them. He threw back another furtive shot of whiskey and looked at his watch. One o'clock. Another early night.

For three years now, Jack had been managing My Wild Irish Rose. He put in long hours behind the bar while Deirdre, his assistant, took care of all the practical details – stock-taking, time sheets, bar shifts – all the stuff Jack had no patience for.

'Jack?' The sound of Danny's voice snapped Jack back to attention. 'What's the story? Are you all closed up here or can we have another drink?' Danny and the woman in the biker jacket were on their second drink.

''Course you can have another drink,' Jack answered.

'But someplace else.'

'So, that's the way it is,' said Danny, pretending to be wounded. 'They suck you in, let you do your "Dancing Bear" routine and then throw you out into the night.'

'You're breaking me heart,' said Jack with a laugh. 'Come here anyway, till I fix you up.'

Danny turned to Jazz. 'Excuse me for a moment, I just have to get X-rayed.'

'Get what?'

'X-rayed. Rhymes with paid.'

Jazz smiled and nodded.

Danny walked over to where Jack stood behind the bar counting out a bundle of notes.

'Here you go,' he said, handing Danny the pile. Danny looked at the bundle: it came to roughly a hundred dollars.

'Are you sure you can afford this much, Jack? Tonight wasn't exactly busy.'

'What are you? Some kind of a saint?' Jack asked. 'You earned it. Every punter in here tonight went home happy and they'll all be back. That's worth a hundred dollars to me, so cut the rockstar with a conscience act and tell me about your new friend down the bar.'

Danny slipped the wad in his pocket and leaned towards Jack over the bar. 'I know you're not going to believe this,' he said quietly, 'but she's a cop.'

'A cop!' Jack looked like he'd been smacked in the face.

'Yeah, a cop. She says she's with the Anti-Crime Unit and that she cruises around in plainclothes preventing crimes before they happen. Ever hear of them?'

Jack nodded. 'Sure, I have. But I wouldn't have pegged her as a cop in a million years. Not even in Anti-Crime. Is she carrying a piece?'

Danny frowned. 'A what?'

'A piece. A gun?' Jack explained.

'Haven't a clue. Anyway, her name's Jazz and I'm going to ask her if she wants to go on somewhere else for a drink. D'you want to come?'

'You're getting your rocks off on going drinking with a cop, aren't you?' Jack teased.

Danny grinned sheepishly. 'Yeah. I'm a sucker for the hint of sleaze and a bit of danger.' He looked down the bar at her. 'A bit of a babe, isn't she?'

Jack just nodded. 'Where are you thinking of going?'

'How about The Buzz? It's a real trendy place owned by a couple of Irish guys.'

'Yeah,' said Jack. 'I've heard of it. Why not so? But see what the lady says first of all.'

Danny walked back to Jazz and sat down. 'Sorry 'bout that. Business had to be done.'

'No problem,' she said.

'Listen, Jazz, myself and Jack are going uptown for a drink. D'you fancy coming?'

A shadow of doubt flickered across her face.

'Hey, Jazz, no strings attached,' Danny said quickly. 'You can leave whenever you want.'

'It's not that, it's just –'

'Just what?'

She looked at Danny and slowly her face softened into a smile. 'Just nothing.'

The traffic was light as Jack nosed his car on to the wide expanse of First Avenue. It had rained and the neon bar and restaurant signs were reflected in the slick black surface of the road. Danny loved New York at this time of night. Even the seediest-looking places promised mystery and adventure.

He reached into his pocket. 'I suppose if I lit a joint you'd have to arrest me?' Danny looked around for Jazz's reaction. She was sucking on a cigarette in the back seat.

'*I* don't give a shit,' she answered, 'but it might look bad if somebody was to pull us over.'

'That sounds like a no to me,' said Danny, sticking the pre-rolled joint back into his jacket pocket.

'Like I say, I don't give a shit about nobody else smoking dope. But I don't, I could lose my job, that's all.'

'What d'you mean?'

'I'm a cop. We're tested for drugs all the time and marijuana stays in your system ninety days, so I can never take the chance.'

'Danny tells me you're with the Anti-Crime Unit,' Jack said over his shoulder. 'What precinct?'

'Midtown North.'

'Jesus, tough area. Are you all the way over on the West side?'

'Yep.'

'Lot of crack over there.'

'You said it.' Jazz obviously didn't like discussing work.

'Lot of hookers too,' Jack persisted.

'Tell me about it. Why d'you think I'm dressed like this?'

'So this isn't the *real* you I'm taking out for a drink?' Danny teased.

Jazz just gave him a cool look and blew a stream of cigarette smoke in his direction.

Danny smiled. 'What does the real Jazz Mahony look like then?'

'She wears different coloured leggings,' she said deadpan.

Danny ducked into a doorway as they walked towards The Buzz. He pulled the joint out of his jacket pocket again, lit it quickly and called to Jack and Jazz to keep on walking ahead. He took three enormous drags from the joint and held all the smoke in. Then he pinched the top from the joint with his thumb and forefinger, flicked it into the gutter and hurried along the sidewalk to catch up with them as they walked through the door.

The place was stuffed with trendies. Danny took a quick look around and then led the way through the throng to the bar. The countertop and all the walls were mirrored glass and with their polished chrome fittings gave an impression of high-tech hip. Bottles of coloured liqueurs, lit from behind, formed a backdrop of lurid colours while the jukebox blared out hip-hop at top volume.

'I'm buying,' Danny volunteered. 'What are you having?' He looked at Jazz. 'No, don't tell me – a Rolling Rock?' Jazz laughed and nodded.

'And a Jameson and water for me,' Jack shouted over the din. 'C'mon, Jazz,' he added, 'let's find a quieter spot to stand in.'

Danny tried to catch the eye of his friend, Robbie Dunne, who was working frantically behind the bar. At last Robbie saw him and his face broke into a wide grin. He reached a hand over the bar. 'Ireland's Most Controversial Rockstar! This is an honour.'

'And Ireland's hippest bar owner. How's it going?' They shook hands.

'Are you here to do Madison Square Garden or is this just a social visit?' Robbie asked, taking orders from other customers as he talked.

Danny laughed. 'Would you believe a Tuesday night gig in My Wild Irish Rose and a shiteload of hustling my songs during the day?'

'What's happened to Poison Pig then?'

The smile disappeared from Danny's face. 'We broke up after Richie overdosed.'

Robbie grimaced. 'Yeah, I heard about Richie. Bad story. You nearly made it big though, didn't you?'

'Yeah. Well, that's rock 'n' roll for you.' Danny shrugged. All that seemed a long time ago to him now.

'Anyway, I'm going to make it here instead. I've a meeting in King Records tomorrow, so I'll probably be rich and famous by next week.'

Danny gave Robbie their order and the drinks were plonked on the counter. 'This one's on me,' said Robbie.

'Thanks. Where's the other eejit?'

'Eamonn? Oh, you know him, I work and he plays. Actually, it's his birthday today and he's been out celebrating. He should be here any moment.'

Jazz watched Danny fight his way to her side with the drinks. She liked the way he moved his six foot frame, limber like an athlete. He was definitely handsome, with that strong Irish face and mane of dark hair.

'So, what d'you think?' Danny shouted to Jazz.

'It's all right,' she shouted back. 'It's a bar.'

'Pardon me,' Danny said. 'I'm just a pooer Irish immigrant who isn't used to all your fancy Noo Yawk bars.'

Jazz laughed at Danny's imitation of her accent. If only Vinny was like him, she thought. Vinny didn't laugh very much. Tonight they had had one of their worst rows ever over the usual small-fry stuff. It seemed the more he worked away from home, the worse things got between them. Funny, she thought, all that stuff about absence making the heart grow fonder was just so much bullshit.

She could still hear his harsh insults echoing in her head and she was glad she had stamped out in a temper. The look of disbelief on his face had been worth it. Seeing My Wild Irish Rose as she rode around in a taxi and deciding to stop for a drink had been a snap decision. But it seemed like a stroke of good fortune now and she was happy to enjoy it.

She tilted the bottle of Rolling Rock to her lips and whispered softly, 'Screw you, Vinny.'

CHAPTER 3

Eamonn Doherty entered The Buzz surrounded by a band of birthday revellers. It could have been a scene from a movie. He stepped naturally into the glare of a spotlamp and waved to those who knew him, a wide smile on his round face. He beamed at the bustle of his crowded bar.

Danny smiled. Still the same old Eamonn. His wide-shouldered suit and loud tie lent him the appearance of an old-style gangster and, on his five feet eight inches, looked wildly inappropriate.

Eamonn scanned the bar. His face registered happy surprise when he finally noticed Danny. He threw him a conspiratorial wink and rubbed the side of his nose with his forefinger. Danny remembered clearly the last time Eamonn had rubbed the side of his nose. They had spent two days in Dublin out of their faces on some of the best coke Danny had ever snorted. A bit more of the same would be very welcome.

Eamonn pointed to a burly guy in a lumberjack shirt. He whispered in the big guy's ear and motioned to Danny to follow the lumberjack shirt.

Danny thought for a moment. No point in inviting Jazz along, not after their conversation in the car. And he could see Jack wedged in at the bar ordering the next round. Danny excused himself to Jazz and followed the lumber-jack shirt as nonchalantly as he could. When he rounded the end of the bar, the guy was holding the door of the Men's open. He ushered Danny inside, then followed him in and bolted the door.

The toilet was meant to accommodate one person at a time, with just a throne and a wash-hand basin stuck on to yet another mirrored wall. Danny thought of himself as being big, but this guy had him dwarfed. He was at least six feet four and almost as wide. Danny grinned.

But the temptation to laugh was stifled by a growl from the monster. 'I don't know you,' he ground out. 'But if you're a cop, I'll come back and find you and I will kill you.' Each syllable was laden with menace.

Danny was taken aback. He looked for a twinkle in the big guy's eye, some sign that he was joking, but all he could discern was a hostile stare.

'Don't be stupid, I'm not a cop,' Danny said, laughing nervously.

The guy prodded him with a fat finger. 'If I lose my job, I'll come back and find you and kill you, even if it takes me forever,' he repeated.

Danny was no longer in any doubt about the seriousness of the threat being made. He watched fascinated as the guy took a huge Swiss Army knife from his back pocket. He pulled out the biggest blade on the knife and Danny gazed as he reached into his shirt pocket and took out a fat envelope. He lifted the flap and suddenly Danny was looking at more coke than he had ever seen in his life.

The monster dipped the knife into the envelope, lifted out a small mound of cocaine on the flat of the blade and rammed the blade under Danny's right nostril. The point of the knife bit into the sensitive skin inside Danny's nose and he recoiled, almost scattering the coke.

'You're spilling it, asshole.'

Danny was in a sweat. He caught a glimpse in the mirror of the pair of them squashed face-to-face in this tiny cubicle. They looked ridiculous, but Danny had no desire to laugh any more. He pushed his left nostril closed with his finger and sniffed as hard as he could. Only half the coke went up his nose.

'Jesus fuckin' Christ! What the fuck is going on?' the guy snarled.

Danny snorted again quickly. He was overcome with relief to see that the blade was almost clean. But it was only a temporary respite. The same procedure had to be gone through with his left nostril.

Danny sniffed as hard as he could in the aftermath to make sure he had ingested all the coke. It was more than he had ever had before in one go, but right now he was concentrating on getting out of the situation without damaging anything more than his brain.

His supplier hoovered up two huge mounds from the tip of the knife himself. Then he wet his finger and wiped the residue from the blade. He rubbed it vigorously into his gums, flicked the blade back into place, folded the flap on the envelope and returned it to his pocket.

'Remember what I told you,' he grunted, fingering the now closed knife. 'If I get busted, I'll find you and kill you.'

'You don't have to worry about me.' Danny was dismayed to hear his voice coming out as a squeak.

'Okay, let's go.' He reached behind Danny and flushed the toilet. Then he slipped the bolt on the door, opened it and stepped quickly out. Danny stood frozen in the open doorway.

'Hey, Irish, how you doing?' It was Jazz.

Danny looked hard at her. What was she doing hanging around outside the Men's and how long she had been there?

'I'm doing fine,' he said slowly. 'Just fine.'

'Good deal,' she said. 'Me too. Come on, your friend will think we've abandoned him.'

'Don't worry about Jack,' Danny said, recovering his composure. 'He's the sort of guy who can handle himself.'

Danny had thought the same about himself. Now he

wasn't so sure. They pushed their way back to where Jack was sitting, nursing a whiskey.

'We was worried you might have thought we'd abandoned you,' Jazz said to Jack.

'Och, I knew you were up to some devilment.'

'It was a majority decision to come back,' Danny heard himself say, 'and I didn't vote.'

Jack laughed and handed Danny his drink. The coke began to kick into Danny's system. His legs felt suddenly weak, his heartbeat accelerated. Everything was turning into a huge rush as though every bit of fluid in his body was trying to find its way to his head.

'Will you excuse me for a minute, guys?' Jazz said. 'I just have to make a quick call.'

'Sure, sure,' said Danny, thrilled to get a chance to offload the experience to Jack. The words tumbled out in a torrent as Danny told him about his encounter in the toilet. By the time he described the sight of the two of them in the mirror, Jack was laughing heartily and Danny found himself smiling in spite of himself.

'Jesus though, Jack, it was no joke all the same. I know I came to New York looking for adventure, but not that fucking fast.' Danny broke off. Over Jack's shoulder he could see the big ape glaring at him. Maybe he was just being paranoid, Danny thought, trying to comfort himself.

'I'll tell you something, Jack,' he continued. 'I'm very stoned and I'm going to be talking twenty to the dozen, but swear you won't say anything to Jazz.'

'No problem,' Jack assured him.

'What do you make of her?' he said, desperate to change the subject.

'Very New York. But there's something sweet about her.'

'Well, back right off, Mr Sweetness,' Danny laughed. 'She's mine.'

The birthday boy, Eamonn, joined them, a huge smile on his face. He grabbed Danny in a bear hug and lifted him – all six foot of him – off the floor. 'Get up, ye boy ye!' he shouted.

'How the fuck are ye, ye Northern bollocks? And happy birthday,' Danny said in a Belfast accent. 'This is my friend, Jack Killoran, who manages My Wild Irish Rose down on Second.'

Eamonn took Jack's outstretched hand. 'I think we might know each other to see,' he said. He gave Jack a long hard look as he shook his hand. There was a pause.

'So what are you up to?' Eamonn asked, turning back to Danny.

'Up to me balls in debt,' said Danny. 'I'm doing a few gigs for Jack here and trying to hustle a few demos during the day.'

Danny didn't pay much attention to the police sirens blaring over the sound of the jukebox, until two sets of flashing blue lights came to a screeching halt outside. He looked out the window and saw four cops, guns drawn, running towards the door. Simultaneously he heard a commotion inside the door. The big guy who had given him the coke was being pushed up against the wall by two men in baseball jackets, his arms and legs spreadeagled as one of the men frisked him.

'What the fuck is going on?' Danny shouted over the noise.

'Don't move,' hissed Eamonn. 'Stay right where you are and don't move. It's a bust. Just stay calm.'

'Yeah, don't move,' Jack said nervously.

Danny looked at Jack and saw that both he and Eamonn had managed to angle their bodies so that only their backs were visible to the uniformed and plainclothes cops. The burly guy's hands were now handcuffed behind his back and as the cops shoved him towards the door, he spun his head and looked straight at Danny.

'You bastard!' he roared. 'I'll get you! You fuckin' set me up! I'll fuckin' ...' His voice tailed off as he was bundled out the door and into the back of one of the police cars. Robbie followed the police out, arguing with one of the officers.

Danny felt a cold pang of fear in his stomach. His eyes were wide with alarm. 'Eamonn, he thinks I set him up.'

The whole bar was staring at him. They seemed to have come to the same conclusion.

'Don't worry. It'll be all right,' Eamonn said, keeping his back to the door.

'No, it won't.' Danny was panicked. 'He threatened me when he was giving me the coke in the jacks. He thinks I set him up. Jesus, Jack will tell you, I came straight back here, didn't I, Jack? I was with Jazz from the minute I left the toilet.'

'Jazz?' said Eamonn. 'Who's Jazz?'

Someone fed the jukebox a quarter and another high decibel track blared out. This evening's floorshow was over.

'The girl who's with us,' Danny said. 'She just went to make a call.' As Danny said it, a horrible thought struck him. Holy shit! It could have been Jazz who phoned the cops. He was suddenly desperate to leave. Mother of Jesus, what a big fucking eejit. She set me up.

The fear was etched into Danny's face. 'Are you all right?' asked Jack.

'What would you think?' Danny replied, his heart pounding. 'Listen, Eamonn, the big guy, he's your friend, isn't he? What's his name?'

'McNally. Dave McNally.'

Danny grabbed Eamonn's arm. 'You'll tell him I had nothing to do with the bust? He thinks I'm a cop!'

Eamonn looked at him. 'He thinks *you're* a cop? *He's* a cop! A mad bastard.'

'What? Oh Jesus,' Danny whispered.

'Jeez, that was some commotion.' Jazz's voice startled Danny. 'What was all that about?' she asked innocently.

'It was a drug bust,' Danny said tersely, trying to read her expression for any sign that would give her away. 'Jazz, this is Eamonn, one of the owners here.'

'How you doing?' Jazz said calmly.

Eamonn nodded briefly in reply.

'I think we should drink up and get out of here,' Jack said.

Danny pulled nervously at his upper lip, as if trying to make up his mind what to do. 'Yeah. Yeah. Let's go. Are you ready, Jazz?'

'Hey, if you want to go, you want to go,' she answered, gulping back her beer.

Danny turned once more to Eamonn. 'You won't forget to tell your pal, will you?'

'I told you I wouldn't,' Eamonn said flatly. 'See you later.' All trace of the happy birthday boy had vanished.

CHAPTER 4

Danny stepped out on to the street. The cold New York wind pierced his face like a thousand microfine needles. He gave an involuntary shudder and hunched his shoulders. Up to this moment the cold had been a normal part of living in New York, something to grumble about good-naturedly. Now it had turned malevolent, an evil force trying to cause him pain.

The smell of fear hung in Danny's nostrils, a pungent odour. He could still see that wild angry face shouting at him. He didn't doubt for a minute that McNally was serious. Half an hour ago he had been enjoying a friendly drink in friendly surroundings. Now, his life had taken a swift turn off the main drag and he was into alien territory, playing a game whose rules he didn't know.

'Are you all right?' Danny felt Jazz's hand on his shoulder.

He shrugged it off and blew on his hands against the cold.

'Yeah, yeah, I'm fine,' he lied.

'Danny, d'you want to go for a drink somewhere else?' asked Jack.

Danny tried to take a deep breath. The coke was well into his system now, its effects heightened by the adrenaline running through his body. Small waves of panic washed over him, making his breath come in shallow gasps.

'I think I'd better go home,' he heard himself say.

'Sure enough,' Jack said. 'C'mon then. Let's go.'

The three of them walked to Jack's car in silence. Danny sat slumped into the front seat as Jack pulled away.

'Jeez, it's cold,' Jazz said.

'Sure is,' Jack agreed, trying hard to inject a tone of normality back into the conversation. 'You don't get this kind of cold back in Dublin, sure you don't, Danny?'

But Danny could think of nothing but that evening's events. 'D'you think the guy was serious?' Danny turned and looked straight at Jazz as he asked the question.

'Nah. He's probably full of shit. You'll never see the creep again. Forget about him.'

'It's easy for you to say that,' Danny snapped, his eyes still locked on to Jazz's face. 'It's not your life he's threatening. It's mine.'

'Listen, the jerk was busted. He has enough to worry about already,' Jazz said.

'Did you know he was a cop?'

''Course I didn't. I never seen the creep before.'

Danny stared straight ahead of him. 'Will you drop me home first please, Jack,' he said quietly.

'Yeah, no problem,' Jack answered. 'Is that all right with you, Jazz?'

'Sure.'

They drove in silence until Jack swung the car on to East Sixth Street.

'Don't worry, Danny,' Jack said. 'All these guys are full of hot air. Your man will be so busy trying to get out on bail that he won't have time to bother looking for you.'

'Just here,' Danny said, indicating to Jack to pull over.

He opened the car door and put one foot on the pavement.

'Hey, Irish!'

Danny turned to Jazz.

'Give me your phone number.'

Danny looked at her balefully.

'Jeez, c'mon. I'm only trying to be friendly here.' She reached out and put her hand on Danny's arm.

He studied her intently. She seemed sincere. 'Okay,' he said reluctantly. He pulled a pen from his pocket and scrawled his number on the flap of an envelope that was in his jacket.

'I'll give you a call tomorrow.'

'Whatever,' he said, letting out a heavy sigh. 'Thanks for the lift, Jack.'

Danny got out and retrieved his guitar from the trunk of the car.

'Will you call me tomorrow, about lunchtime?' said Jack. 'We can organise your next gig.'

'I will, yeah.'

Danny trudged up the two flights of stairs to his apartment. He turned the keys in the three different locks and pushed the door open. Earlier he had been laughing and joking with Jazz about how paranoid everybody was in New York. Now, as he closed the door behind him, he was glad of the security.

The apartment was in darkness except for the panel light on the cooker. Danny wasn't sure what he needed or wanted. Right now a cup of tea would have to do. An Irish solution. It would give him time to think. The apartment was warm, but Danny felt a cold clammy hand on his heart. A hot cup of tea would definitely make him feel better.

He put the kettle on and went to the fridge to get milk. He opened the door and the first thing he saw was a handwritten note on the middle shelf. It was sitting on top of a plate which had a leg of chicken on it.

Danny picked up the note. It wasn't addressed to anyone in particular.

> Some of us in this apartment are vegetarians. It would help if those who are not could avoid leaving animal products exposed in the refrigerator.
> Thank you

'*Jesus vegetarian fucking Christ!*' Danny's first reaction

was to kick open Gail's bedroom door. But in spite of his anger he had to smile. That butch bitch Gail was probably as dangerous as McNally, he thought. She ruled the apartment, hogged the biggest bedroom, filled the fridge with alfalfa and neither himself nor Anton, the other inhabitant, was brave enough to protest. New York was doing it to him big time. Not only did he have a bent cop threatening to kill him, but now a vegetarian vigilante was on to him for leaving a chicken leg exposed.

Danny took the cup of hot tea and made his way to the sofa in the sittingroom. Since he had moved in a month ago, he had spent most of his time in the apartment in the confines of his own room, the smallest bedroom. It overlooked East Sixth Street and his nights were punctuated with the clanking of garbage trucks and the banshee wails of police and ambulance sirens.

Gail and Anton also kept to their rooms and Danny didn't blame them. The drab carpet and ageing white walls of the sittingroom were not conducive to relaxation. Apart from the sofa, there was only one armchair and a scattering of other pieces of tacky furniture. A cheap black and white TV sat on the table which divided the sittingroom and the kitchen and this was where Danny usually ate.

He sat in the dark and tried to make sense of the night. From the moment Eamonn had given him the wink everything had gone incredibly wrong. The acrid taste of the coke was still in the back of his nose and throat and his whole body was fizzing like a freshly opened bottle of soda. He pulled the roach of the joint he had been smoking earlier, lit it and inhaled deeply. Maybe the grass would calm him down.

He looked at his watch. It was still too early to think of ringing anyone in Ireland. Not that he had anyone to call. Mary had made it clear when he left that she didn't want him bothering her or the kids. And his dad? Well, they hadn't got beyond small talk in years.

The grass was making Danny edgy instead of tranquillising him. He got up and went to the television and turned it on. Blizzards of interference blotted out the picture. He flicked through the channels. The only thing half-visible was a re-run of 'Sergeant Bilko' and after two minutes he realised that even Phil Silvers wasn't enough to distract him.

He went into his room and switched on the light. Stupid American switches, he thought. You have to push them up to turn them on.

'Fuck you, America,' he muttered.

Danny brought his guitar in from the sittingroom, took it from its case and began to strum it vigorously.

> I'm stuck in this goddamn awful place
> Fuck you, America
> I might as well be in outer space
> Fuck you, America ...

He closed his eyes and sang the same four lines over and over, accompanying them with a jerky riff, which hypnotised him as he repeated it. Danny forgot where he was until the sound of irate knocking on the ceiling of the apartment below brought him out of his spell.

He realised that Gail mustn't be home, otherwise she would have come in from the bedroom next door by now. What was he supposed to do now – sleep? That wasn't going to be easy.

'Ah, fuck me,' Danny said through gritted teeth. He lifted up his mattress and pulled out a small wooden box with 'Emergency' written on the lid. He lifted the lid and looked at his small collection of pills. He had three five-milligram valium, two laxatives and three white halcyon sleeping tablets.

'This is a genuine emergency,' he said aloud and popped a sleeping tablet into his mouth. He packed away his guitar, stripped off down to a T-shirt and boxers, switched out the light and climbed into bed. He lay there, his thoughts careering wildly around like a pinball inside his head. The kaleidoscopic pictures flashed, banged and lit up.

Jazz. Coke. Screaming threats. Chickens with trousers. Police sirens. Eamonn. The Statue of Liberty. A big knife ...

'Hey!'

Danny's heart jumped straight into his mouth with fear. Someone was shaking him by the shoulder. Had the mad cop come for him already?

'Hey, man! There's somebody at the door for you.' Danny looked up and saw his room-mate, Anton, standing over his bed.

'Someone at the door? For me?'

'Yeah, man. And I don't appreciate it one bit at this hour of the night.'

'I'm sorry,' Danny said as he fought the blankets to get out of bed. He flicked on the light. 'I didn't hear the buzzer. Did he say who he was?'

'It's a woman and she says her name is Jazz.'

CHAPTER 5

Danny pulled Jazz inside angrily, relocked the door and took her by the elbow down to his bedroom. She stood awkwardly until Danny motioned her to sit on the bed. He sat down beside her.

'Jazz, what are you doing here?' His voice was full of hostility.

'I had to come and talk to you,' she answered, her eyes pleading for understanding.

'Is that so? Well, you just talked to my room-mate Anton as well and he's not too happy about it.'

'Oh shit.'

'You could've phoned if you wanted to talk that badly.

'Okay, okay. It's more than that.'

'What do you mean, "more than that"?' Could the evening get any worse, Danny wondered.

Jazz glanced at him, then down at her feet and then back up at him again. 'I have nowhere to stay tonight. I thought you might let me stay here.'

Between the coke, the joint and the sleeping tablet, Danny's head was buzzing. He tried to focus on what Jazz was saying. 'What do you mean? Did you lose your keys or something?'

'No.' She hesitated. 'I was locked out.'

'Who locked you out?'

'Vinny.'

'Vinny? Who the hell is Vinny?'

'Vinny is the guy I've been living with for the last year.' Jazz looked at Danny to see his reaction. His expression hovered between disbelief and anger.

Then he exploded. 'So Vinny, your boyfriend, locks you out and you come here!' He shook his head. 'What the fuck is going on, Jazz? You're trouble, you know that? I don't like this one bit.'

'I know you don't. But listen to me for a minute, it's important.'

Danny's eyes were blazing with anger. 'I'm listening.'

'All right. I could have gone and stayed with one of my girlfriends, but I came here because there's more to it than just Vinny.' She seemed relieved to have finally said it.

'More! There's more?' Danny hissed. 'What *more* can there be?'

'The bust tonight – I called it in.'

Danny clutched his head in his hands. 'I fucking knew

it,' he muttered. 'I knew it. I knew it.'

Then he whirled on her. 'Jesus, Jazz, what else are you going to tell me? That you're with the Immigration Department as well and that I'm being deported in the morning?'

'Look, it's not as simple as all that. The guy who was busted is a bent cop. His name is McNally and everybody is afraid of him because the guy is a psycho.'

That was exactly what Eamonn had said, Danny remembered. 'But you said you didn't know him.'

'Yeah, well I had to in front of your friend. I'm sorry, but this is a bad asshole. I know for a fact that he's been hustling free sex from the hookers on my beat and he beats the shit out of them and makes them do really weird stuff.'

She paused for breath, confident now that she had Danny's attention. 'He's also stealing confiscated drugs and selling them back to junkies on the street. When I saw him tonight and saw the two of you go into the toilet, I put two and two together and took a chance on landing him in the shit.'

Danny gave her a cold stare. 'Well, congratulations, it's *me* you landed in the shit.'

'I know that now, but I swear to you I didn't set out to land you in it. And I don't know why he fingered you.'

Danny filled her in on his encounter with McNally in the toilet and the threats he had made.

'Jeez, Danny, I'm really sorry. I really am. If I had of known I wouldn't have done it.'

'Spare me the apologies, Jazz,' Danny said with a sigh.

He gave her a searching look. 'How dangerous is this guy?'

She looked at him for a moment as if making up her mind about something. Then she answered. 'Like I said, he's a psycho. He's beaten up a lot of people and the story on the street is that he whacked a guy from Brooklyn last year, but nobody could prove anything.'

'Whacked?' repeated Danny, his voice climbing an octave. 'You mean *killed*?'

She shifted her gaze from Danny. 'Yeah, I mean killed.'

'Holy shit.' Danny got up and walked around the room. 'What am I supposed to do? Sit here until he comes around and whacks me?'

'Danny, don't panic. He's not going to come around tonight.'

'That's great news. He's going to come around tomorrow night instead.'

'They'll keep him in the slammer as long as they can. The Internal Affairs guys will be called in, so it'll be a few days before he's back on the street. Anyway, he doesn't know where you live, does he?'

'No, he doesn't, but if the guy's any kind of a half-decent cop it won't take him long to find out, will it? Anyway, he knows I'm a friend of Eamonn's and Robbie's.'

'Is there anywhere else you can stay for a few days, until this blows over?'

'Jazz, I don't think you're listening to me. This guy didn't say anything about a few days. He said if it took him forever, he'd get me. Anyway,' Danny said, coming to a halt in front of her, 'I don't have anywhere else to go and I don't have the money to spend on a hotel. I don't have a Green Card either so I'm an illegal alien –'

She put up her hand and stopped him in mid-sentence. 'I don't need to know, so forget you told me. Immigration is somebody else's problem. Give me time to think about it. I'll find you somewhere to stay.'

They were silent for a minute, each of them staring at the ground. Danny finally broke the tension, his eyes still firmly fixed on a point between his feet. 'Look, Jazz, you have Vinny and I have hassles in the domestic department too.'

'What d'you mean?'

'I have a wife and two kids back in Dublin. We're separated at the moment, mostly because I was screwing around. I wasn't getting any work in Dublin either. That's really why I came here – to try and make a few dollars because I'm still supporting them.' He paused awkwardly. 'Anyway, everything else I told you about coming here, you know about trying to get a record deal, that's all true.'

Her gaze softened. 'Hey, I understand. I do, really.'

Jesus, he thought, why didn't I tell her earlier? I might have avoided all this mess.

But even so, even with the death threats of a maniac cop hanging over him, Danny realised he was glad to be here with Jazz. Danny Toner felt alive – one hundred per cent alive.

'So what about Vinny?' Danny said at last sitting down beside her.

'Vinny? Vinny's a jerk,' expostulated Jazz. 'He's Italian, full of all this macho shit.'

'But why did he lock you out?'

Jazz described that evening's row and explained how she'd ended up in My Wild Irish Rose. 'I was riding round in a taxi and I guess something Irish pulled me in there.'

Danny permitted himself a smile. 'Must have been me. But Jesus, Jazz, you sure know how to complicate someone's life.'

'Yours, you mean?'

'Damn right. A couple of hours ago I was a guy looking for a break in the music biz and now I'm locked into some life-threatening psycho-drama and I haven't a fucking clue what to do.'

Jazz reached out, laid her hand on top of Danny's and squeezed it. He looked up at her and she gave him a half-smile. Then she leaned over and planted her generous lips on his mouth in a firm kiss.

Alarm bells clanged in Danny's head. The last thing he needed right now was to get tangled up with another woman. He hesitated for just a second, then drew Jazz towards him and put his arms around her.

'This is another fine mess you got me into, Stanley,' he said.

Jazz pulled back from him and raised her right hand to cradle his face. Then she kissed him, her tongue slipping into his mouth. He sucked her tongue, long and hard, as she manoeuvered her way out of her heavy leather jacket. He laid her gently back on the bed and slid his hand up under her shirt until he touched her breast. The nipple was hard. Danny lifted her shirt up over her breasts and tore his mouth away from hers to plunge it on to her firm brown aureole. She murmured encouragement as Danny sucked one nipple and caressed the other with the tips of his finger.

'Stop for a minute.' Jazz forced her way up to a sitting position. 'Lie back,' she ordered. 'Come on.'

Danny obeyed and Jazz lifted his T-shirt up and began to trace a light line down his chest with her tongue. Danny felt himself go hard as a rock.

Danny kept his eyes closed until every little sensation of pleasure had rippled its way out to the extremities of his body and he felt himself go limp again.

Life couldn't get any stranger. As if the night had not already contained enough adventure, now he had got laid too. He sensed Jazz watching him and opened his eyes.

'Was that good?' she asked, smiling.

'Oh Jesus, was that good?' Jazz had been even wilder than he had imagined, using the bed space like a demented choreographer, dictating every movement, every position, twisting and turning, bending, plunging, sucking, stroking until they had shuddered to a heaving finale, half in and half out of the bed. 'My God, I think I needed that.'

‘That’s why I did it.’ She laughed. ‘D’you think I can stay the night now?’

‘No question. Was that as good as Vinny?’ he added.

‘Men,’ she sighed. ‘You’re all the same. Am I better in the sack than he is? Is mine bigger than his? What’s so important? I came, didn’t I?’

‘Okay, okay. I’m sorry. I just wondered, that’s all. I mean what’s Vinny like? Is he small. Is he tall? Is he tough?’

‘Vinny’s a bit bigger than you and he’s the most jealous guy in the world. He’s very dark and very Italian. And if he thought I was in bed with you, he’d rip my head off and then he’d rip your head off.’

‘You’re joking, aren’t you?’

‘Sure, I’m joking.’

‘Bitch,’ Danny said. ‘You’re winding me up again.’ He pinched her buttock.

‘Hey, watch it,’ she said. ‘No rough stuff.’

Danny laughed and pulled at the duvet until they were both underneath. ‘Hold on. I’ll turn out the lights.’

‘It’s okay.’ She grinned. ‘I’m not shy.’

‘Yeah,’ Danny said. ‘But you never know, we might actually get some sleep.

CHAPTER 6

The sound of heavy knocking woke Jack from a drunken sleep. He shook himself free of the covers and shuffled to the door in his vest and shorts. The safety chain was on. He unhooked it and opened the door without thinking, his natural caution blunted by the throbbing in his head and the sour taste of whiskey in his mouth.

'Still in bed, you lazy fuckin' harp!' The door was kicked in, sending Jack reeling backwards. He blinked and squinted, trying to focus on the man who had burst into his apartment.

'You know me all right, cocksucker,' the intruder jeered. 'It was your little buddy who blew the whistle on me last night. Or were you too fucking drunk to notice?'

Jack sat down heavily on the arm of a chair. He recognised McNally. He was bigger than he remembered him from the night before and his face was contorted in anger.

'Danny didn't finger you,' Jack said. 'I was with him the whole evening.'

'Were you now?' McNally said, reaching down and dragging Jack up by the front of his vest. 'Are you two faggots or something?'

'I'm just telling you that Danny didn't call the cops.'

'Well, somebody did and I think it was your little faggoty friend. Does he live here too?'

'No, he doesn't.'

'So where does he live then?'

'I don't know,' Jack lied.

'I don't know,' mimicked McNally. 'What kind of a turkey do you take me for? 'Course you know.'

'I swear I don't know,' Jack said, trying to keep his voice calm. How the fuck had McNally tracked him down?

McNally's fist exploded into Jack's mouth sending his head crashing against the back of the chair. He felt the blood spurting from his lower lip. More blood trickled down inside his mouth, mixing with the taste of stale whiskey.

'Maybe that'll help you remember.'

Jack looked up at McNally in disgust. The blow was like being doused with cold water. He had been beaten so often in prison and detention centres in Belfast, that the one thing he knew how to do was take physical punishment. Every blow had only stiffened his resolve to divulge nothing, to resist.

'Can I get dressed?' Jack asked.

'No, you can't,' McNally snarled. 'When is this faggot singing again?'

'Next week, probably.'

'Well, do you probably know the day, slobbo? Probably St Paddy's Day? That's this week.'

'Probably Friday next week.'

'You'd better be right, buddy boy, 'cos otherwise I'll be back. And next time I might have to crack your head a little harder.'

Jack stared defiantly at him, hoping McNally could read the disdain in his eyes. The big man hesitated, confused by Jack's lack of fear. He kicked a bottle and it flew across the room and smashed off a wall. Still Jack continued to stare at him unflinchingly. McNally turned and walked to the door.

'Stupid Irish bastard,' he said over his shoulder. 'And clean up this place. It's a fuckin' pigpen.'

Jack didn't move for a while after McNally left. He fingered his bruised lip and lay back in the armchair, letting his mind freewheel. Meeting Eamonn Doherty the night before had knocked him off balance. He knew as soon as Eamonn set eyes on him, that for the first time in years his real identity had been rumbled. Eamonn knew him as Kevin O'Toole, IRA hero.

It brought it all back to him, his escape from Crumlin

Road jail disguised as a priest, the three months he had spent in a safe house in County Clare until he had been spirited into America via Canada with a new name and a set of new identity papers.

No one ever suspected now that Jack Killoran was anything other than a decent Irish bachelor working as a bartender in New York. No one ever knew that the first image he saw when he woke every morning was a spray of blood and bone, followed by some grotesque slow-motion replay, a young soldier falling, his expression a mixture of disbelief and naked fear.

Some days what Jack called the 'Black Fog' would come, lying dark and heavy on his head, while an invisible hand gripped at his heart and squeezed it tight. Then he would call into My Wild Irish Rose pleading sickness, and lie in bed until the fog cleared.

Jack reached automatically for the whiskey bottle he kept stashed away. For a while he had been completely in control of his drink, using it as medication. But as time went on, he knew deep down that he was hooked. The alcohol dulled his senses, it helped him sleep, hours of dream-free blackness, with no bursting heads, no terrified faces, no dull thud of explosions, no funeral processions.

He looked around his apartment and recognised the truth of McNally's final insult. Crumlin Road jail had made Kevin O'Toole neat and tidy, but now his apartment was littered with clothes, newspapers, old take-aways, over-flowing ashtrays and empty bottles. The smell of stale booze hung in the air.

Jack put down the bottle unopened. He got up, reached across the sink and pushed open the grime-encrusted window for the first time in more than a year. A cold blast of air hit him flush in the face and he shivered with the awareness that control of his life was slipping away into hands other than his own.

CHAPTER 7

Danny felt the warm body beside him. It took him a moment to remember where he was. He opened his eyes and saw Jazz sleeping peacefully. He watched her for a while. Then he felt for her nipple and gently caressed it. She opened her eyes and smiled at him.

'It's very sexy to watch someone while they're sleeping,' he murmured.

'That so?' she whispered, pulling him close.

'Wait! Wait a minute,' Danny said scrabbling for his watch. 'Holy fuck! It's ten past ten.'

He jumped out of the bed. 'C'mon, Jazz. I've got to get my shit together and get up to this guy at King Records.'

'Can I stay here?' she asked from the warmth of the bed.

'No, you can't. Gail'd go nuts. And I have to lock the door behind me when I go.'

'Who's Gail?'

Danny filled her in.

'Well, what time will you be finished with that guy?'

'I don't know. I don't know!' Danny tore furiously at the clothes hanging in his small closet.

'Let me stay here. I'm off-duty till tonight,' Jazz coaxed. 'I'll take my chances with Gail. And I'll buy you lunch in O'Grady's later,' she added.

Danny looked at her doubtfully, then relented. 'Okay. Okay.' He grabbed a towel and ran to the bathroom. He showered and shaved hastily and came back rubbing himself dry with the towel.

'Shit, shit, shit, my good shirt is all creases.'

'Relax,' said Jazz from the bed. 'It looks fine. Anyway, you're a rock 'n' roller. It's cool for you to be crumpled.'

'Oh yeah,' Danny said sceptically. He pulled on his jeans, tucked the crumpled shirt in, buttoned his fly and threw on a jacket. 'Will I do?' he asked, combing his hair with his fingers.

'You'll do fine.'

'All right. Wish me luck,' he ordered.

'Good luck, baby.'

Danny blew her a kiss, took a cassette from his table, stuffed it into his inside pocket and left.

He bounced down the two flights of stairs and pushed open the glass door. The day was cold, but sunny. He hurried up Sixth Street, across Avenue A and swung right at First Avenue.

Danny cast a glance along the wide ribbon of cracked and rutted concrete and tarmacadam. Yesterday it had beckoned to him invitingly, today it was a racetrack of rude drivers, honking and swearing at each other.

Danny tried not to think about McNally, but every time he saw a big guy in front of him, he crossed to the other side of the street and ducked past as quickly as he could. He made a mental note to ring Jack as soon as he finished his meeting at the record company and see about finding some safe place to hang out for a few days.

He hurried down into Astor Place station and paced backwards and forwards nervously as he waited for the subway.

As the subway rumbled uptown, Danny ran over his spiel in his mind. He mustn't seem too eager. He must be laidback and cool, as though he was considering several other offers. But King would be a good one to pull, the hottest independent label in America.

Danny looked at his watch as he ran up the steps at Fifty-first Street. Ten to eleven. He broke into a run, dodging in and out between pedestrians. He reached Seventh Avenue in five minutes and slowed to a walk, giving himself some time to get his breath back. He was hot and flustered and he could feel the stickiness of sweat. The last thing he needed was two big damp patches under his arms.

He found the King Records building and scanned the list of companies for the floor number. King Records:

Twenty-first Floor. He joined a crowd getting into the elevator and was whisked silently skywards.

Danny stepped out into a plush lobby with a reception desk. A blond receptionist, chewing gum, talked on the phone. She gave him a cursory glance as he approached the desk but continued with her conversation.

Danny stood listening with interest, she was the only person he had ever heard capable of saying 'Hey!' in so many different ways.

'Hey!' surprised.

'Hey!' reassuring.

'Hey!' threatening.

After what seemed like an age, the blonde said, 'Listen, I'd better go. I'll talk to you later. Hey.'

She replaced the receiver and looked up at Danny. 'Can I help you?'

'I have an appointment with Rick Dawdle,' said Danny nervously. 'At eleven o'clock.'

'And your name?'

'Toner. Danny Toner.'

She pressed a button on her phone intercom. 'Debbie, I have a Danny Tomer here for Rick.'

'Toner,' Danny said exasperatedly. 'T-O-N-E-R.'

A voice crackled back on the speaker. 'Rick's not here yet. I'm expecting him soon. Can you ask him to wait?'

She looked up at Danny. 'You hear that? He's expected soon. Take a seat.'

Danny sat down on the soft black leather couch set

against the end wall of the lobby. They must have the whole floor, he thought. Classy furniture. Big operation. He picked up the copy of *Billboard* which lay on the coffee table in front of the couch. He tried to read it, but the information wasn't going in. Three times the elevator disgorged people, but none of them was Rick Dawdle.

Danny looked at his watch. Eleven-thirty. Bloody typical. He felt like exploding.

The elevator door opened a fourth time and a guy in his mid-thirties ambled out and past the receptionist.

'Good morning, Jaclyn,' he drawled. 'Any messages for me?'

'Hey, Rick! You're to ring Chuck as soon as you get in, and this gentleman, Mr Tomer, is waiting for you.' Rick turned and nodded to Danny.

'Good morning,' said Danny. 'I'm Danny Toner.'

'Oh yeah, you're the Irish guy. What time was our appointment for?'

'Eleven o'clock,' Danny said, trying not to sound annoyed.

'Oh shit, I apologise.' He actually looked sincere. 'Hey man, just let me make this one call and then you can come through.'

He walked down the corridor again and passed through a door. Danny resigned himself to a long wait, but he was scarcely sitting down when the phone rang and Jaclyn gave him directions to the office.

'Thank you,' said Danny.

'Hey!'

He walked down the hall. The third door was open. He knocked and a girl came out from an inner office.

'Mr Toner? In here, please.' She gestured towards the inner office.

Danny stepped inside. He took a quick glance around. A corner office – a mark of respect in big status-symbol country. Rick Dawdle sat behind a huge desk. Behind him floor-to-ceiling windows looked out over Manhattan to the Hudson River. It was the first time Danny had been this high up since he had flown into New York.

'That's quite a view.'

'Yeah,' Rick Dawdle grinned. 'Day after day after day after day. Sit down, Danny.'

Danny was pleased. The man seemed to be friendly, nice open smile, sense of humour. At least he had apologised for being late. Danny had lost count of the number of A & R toads who had left him waiting for hours and then treated him like shit.

'So what's your story, Danny? This your first time in New York?' Rick lit up a cigarette and put his feet up on the desk in front of him.

'No,' said Danny beginning to relax himself. 'I was here about seven years ago with an Irish folk group.'

'And where did you sing?'

'Up in the Bronx mostly, but to tell you the truth I didn't enjoy it much.'

'Why's that?'

'Well, I might as well still have been in Ireland. I was stuck with Irish people morning, noon and night. And I had to sing all this political Irish shit. It's not that I'm not proud to be Irish or anything like that, it's just that ...' Danny trailed off.

'You don't have to worry about what I think,' Rick said, laughing. 'I'm just about the only person I know in New York who doesn't have any Irish relations.' Danny heaved a sigh of relief.

'So what did you do back in Ireland?' Rick went on.

As succinctly as he could, Danny filled Rick in on the career of Poison Pig, his rock band. Since their bass player died of a heroin overdose on the brink of a major deal Danny had played with different bands and worked on making demos of his own songs.

Rick nodded. 'Do you have a tape?'

'I do, yeah,' Danny said, fumbling in his inside jacket pocket for his cassette.

The office was uncomfortably warm, and Danny fought to keep his composure as his cassette was placed in the player. The music welled out into the room and Danny turned his eyes to the floor. He hated this moment. He never knew where to look. It's like being on the fucking subway, he thought, you try to avoid making eye contact whatever you do.

Instead he concentrated on trying to read, upside down, the sleeve of the album that lay on the desk in front of him. Then he examined his brown brogues and congratulated himself again on overcoming the middle-class sensibilities which had almost prevented him from accepting a gift from Manhattan.

The first song finished.

'I like that. I like your voice,' said Rick. He sat back and joined his hands under his chin as the second song boomed out.

Danny went through three more minutes of squirming and then Rick got up, walked across the room and clicked the cassette machine off. 'So, Danny, you're not tied to anybody for management or for publishing?'

'No,' Danny confirmed. Be cool, stay calm, he told himself.

'And there are no messy deals in the past?' Rick asked, swinging his legs down and leaning forward towards Danny.

'No.'

'Okay. Well, Danny, I like what I hear and I'll play it at our A & R meeting on Monday.'

Danny took this as the cue to stand up. The executive came round his desk and held out his hand. Danny liked his firm handshake.

'Thanks for coming in, Danny. We'll be in touch next week.'

'Thanks,' said Danny, a bit stunned. 'Thanks a lot.' He turned and walked out of the office and back down the corridor to the lobby. He pressed the elevator button and stood back to wait. It had been a good meeting.

The blond receptionist was filing her nails and didn't even look up as the bell rang to indicate that the elevator had arrived. Danny stepped inside and just as the doors closed shouted, 'Hey!'

CHAPTER 8

There was a spring in Danny's step as he pushed his way through the door of O'Grady's Bar and Restaurant. He scanned the place for Jazz and finally spotted her in the darkest corner of the restaurant.

The hostess led him over to Jazz's table. He noticed that Jazz had changed her clothes and was now wearing a shocking-red mini skirt, a matching shirt under her leather jacket and a pair of very dark sunglasses. Was this the real Jazz, he wondered, or another cop outfit?

'Hi,' she said.

'Are you expecting a lot of sunshine?' asked Danny as he sat down.

'Not really.' She sounded subdued.

'Is there something the matter, Jazz?'

'No. No. It's okay.'

'No, it's not okay. I see you changed your clothes.'

She didn't answer.

'Does that mean you went back to Vinny's place? Wait, don't tell me – you and Vinny had a bad row?'

Jazz didn't answer, but Danny saw a tear rolling down from under the dark glasses. He reached across and took the glasses from her face. Her right eye was puffy, red and angry-looking. He could see bruising beginning to appear.

'The bastard hit you! Jazz, what happened? C'mon, tell me. What happened?'

She sniffed and wiped her nose with her napkin. 'I went by the apartment and I didn't see his car in the parking lot, so I thought he was out. I was wrong. He was waiting there and he just freaked out and started slapping me around.'

'Hold on here, didn't you remind the asshole that he was the one who locked you out?'

'Yeah, I did, but he said I should've woke him up.'

'Where did you say you spent the night?' Danny asked anxiously.

'I wouldn't tell him and that's when he gave me this.' She pointed to her swollen eye.

'Did you tell him after he punched you?'

'I had to. He was going crazy – but I didn't say we slept together or anything.'

'But he assumes we did anyway?'

'Yeah. I suppose,' she said in a subdued voice.

Danny sighed. 'I need a drink.' He called the waitress. 'Can I have a Black Jack and Coke please and a Rolling

Rock.' He looked at Jazz, but he couldn't read her expression behind the dark glasses. 'This is getting weirder by the minute, Jazz. I mean, what happens next?'

'I don't know,' she sighed.

'Did he ever hit you before?'

'No.'

'Where's Vinny now?'

'He stormed out, so I grabbed some clothes and dropped them up at the precinct house on my way here.'

'So you're not going back there?'

'No way! That piece of shit.' She sounded angry now.

'Okay, okay. Don't worry. We'll figure something out.'

Jazz reached across and took Danny's hand in hers and squeezed it.

'Okay, plan of action,' Danny said, glancing at the menu. 'You order me a House Special Burger and fries and whatever you're having yourself. I'll go and call Jack like I promised.'

The worry on Danny's face was visible to Jazz as he walked back to the table after phoning Jack. She felt really bad about what was happening. Not alone had she put him in danger from McNally, but now he had Vinny gunning for him as well.

'Danny, I'm really sorry, I forgot to ask you how you got on this morning.'

Jazz's news had pushed it to the back of Danny's mind

too. 'Don't worry about it,' he said grimly. 'I'll tell you later.' There were more serious matters to deal with.

'What is it?'

'McNally is back on the street,' Danny replied.

'Already!' Jazz frowned. This was definitely not normal police procedure.

'Yeah, already. Jack reckons he must be able to pull strings, maybe someone higher up is looking after him.' He took a gulp of his drink. 'He beat Jack up, trying to find out where I live.'

'Oh shit. Did he tell McNally?'

'No, thank God. But he thinks I should lie low. And the Paddy's Day gig is off – McNally is much too interested in my next appearance.'

The food arrived at the table. Danny picked at his fries and nibbled at the burger. Jazz toyed with her food as well. Neither of them spoke for several minutes, until Jazz took off her sunglasses and looked him straight in the eye. 'Danny, you could run home to Ireland right now, today.'

The thought had occurred to Danny too, but he had dismissed it. This was make or break for him.

Jazz watched as Danny weighed up the situation again in his mind. When he spoke his voice was firm. 'Fuck this, Jazz,' he explained. 'I'm scared shitless of McNally, but I've only been here a few weeks and I can't go running home already. I had a really good meeting with that guy in King Records this morning, so anything could happen. I mean, that's what I came here for. I can't just walk away from it because some big galoot wants to shoot my fucking head off.'

She looked at him, her face full of concern, but Danny began to laugh, realising what an indignant rant had come tumbling out. 'Do you think I should call Steven Spielberg and tell him I'm ready to do *Indiana Toner and the Raiders of the Lost Narc*?'

Jazz broke into a smile. 'You're crazy, Irish. That's what you are. Crazy.'

CHAPTER 9

Eamonn Doherty shifted uneasily on his stool as he toyed with his bottle of beer. He didn't like The Crooked Shillelagh, he didn't like the Bronx and he particularly didn't like Bainbridge Avenue. It brought back awful memories of his first few months in America when he had worked for slave wages as a bartender in a dingy neighbourhood bar called O'Rourke's.

He had left Belfast thinking that anywhere else would be a better and a safer place to live. The fact that one of his brothers had been killed in a raid on a British Army barracks and another was in The Maze, left Eamonn an impossible legacy to live up to. The only way was out.

But Eamonn had found that there was no way out. The Bronx was as bad a ghetto as West Belfast. Sloganeering and anti-British jingoism were all around him. He'd moved out of the Bronx and into Manhattan as soon as he could.

And now Kevin O'Toole – or Jack Killoran as he called himself – had popped up. It was just as his father had said, 'You'll never leave Belfast behind, Eamonn.'

The last thing Eamonn needed now was this gorilla McNally running out of control.

He got up from his stool and walked across to the phone to dial The Buzz. He got Robbie on the phone.

'Eamonn. What's happening?'

'Nothing yet. This fucker hasn't shown up and I've been waiting a half-hour.'

Eamonn stiffened as he felt something poking into the small of his back. 'This fucker is here now.' He turned and looked up at McNally, who towered over him. He was laughing viciously as he held up the two fingers that he had poked into Eamonn's back. 'Bet that scared the crap out of you.'

'Big joke,' Eamonn said. 'I'm sitting over there at the bar.' He pointed to his stool.

'Oh,' jeered McNally, 'is it a private conversation?'

'Yes, it is,' Eamonn said coldly.

'Hey, fuck you if you can't take a joke. I'm putting a drink on your tab.'

Eamonn waited until McNally walked over to the bar. Then he asked Robbie what he'd heard.

'Not a word on Danny yet. I've rung around all over and nobody's seen him.'

'Shit.'

'I have to tell you, Eamonn, I'm not too happy about putting McNally on Danny's tail. Danny never did anything to us and I'm nearly certain that he had nothing to do with the bust. Sure he was barely in the door at the time.'

But someone had fingered McNally, and he seemed convinced it was Danny. The pressure was on to find him and deliver him to McNally. And to add a little urgency to the matter McNally was threatening Robbie's and Eamonn's business.

'What d'you mean "threatening us"?' Robbie had asked. Eamonn repeated what McNally had hinted: he couldn't guarantee his friends' good behaviour next time they visited The Buzz – sometimes his boys got a little wild. That and the drug squad's recent interest in their business added up to more heat than Eamonn wanted.

'Robbie,' said Eamonn, eyeing McNally nervously, 'I'll talk to you again as soon as I've finished with King fucking Kong. Good luck.'

Eamonn was conscious of McNally watching him as he walked back across the bar and sat down on his stool. He felt dwarfed beside him but he tried not to let his fear show.

'So what have you found out for me?' McNally asked.

'Nothing so far.'

'Nothing! Who is this guy? Houdini? He's Irish, isn't he? Somebody must know him.'

'You don't understand. Danny Toner's not like your regular Irish guy. This guy is a rock singer and he doesn't hang out in the Irish bars. He's only been here a few weeks, so nobody has seen him more than once and nobody knows where he's living.'

'I bet that fucker Killoran does.'

'Jack?'

'Yeah, that guy who manages My Wild Irish Rose. I paid the cocksucker a visit, but he says he doesn't know where he lives, so I slapped him 'round a bit and told him I'd be back.' McNally guffawed at the memory.

'Slapped him 'round?' Eamonn repeated anxiously.

'Relax, relax,' McNally said. 'I just gave him a fat lip this time, but I might have to go back and really work him over.'

Eamonn felt a moment of panic at the mention of Jack's name. If McNally got his teeth into him and attracted any attention Jack could easily wind up being extradited to Northern Ireland. That long moment of silence the night before when he and Jack had met again had covered a mass of emotions – and memories. Jack had taken a bullet meant for Eamonn's brother Michael years ago. It was a waste of effort – Michael was long since dead, killed in the Army barracks raid, but even so Eamonn couldn't stop himself from feeling he owed Jack a certain loyalty.

'Jack's a mouse,' Eamonn said. 'He couldn't say boo to a goose. If he didn't tell you this time, then he doesn't know.'

'Yeah? Well, Toner is probably playing St Paddy's Day as well. Though that prick told me he wouldn't be back until late next week. Anyway, even if I have to wait a few days, I'll get him.'

'Dave,' Eamonn said, trying to reason with him. 'Do you not think you'd be better off forgetting about Toner? I mean, you don't need the heat and if you rough him up, you might just get in more trouble.'

'The jerk's an illegal alien, so he ain't even officially here. When they find him, he'll be unrecognisable.'

Eamonn flinched, the guy was a lunatic. 'And what if he wasn't the one who set you up?'

'Fuck him. Now business. How much d'you want this week? Two grammes?'

'None,' Eamonn said hesitantly. 'I've decided to ease back a bit.'

McNally glared at him. 'You're going to ease back? Ease back, my ass,' he said, his voice loaded with menace, his brows furrowed with anger. 'One little bust and you're running home to Mommy. You were happy enough to have it for your birthday. No way, Eamonn. You're in for your usual two grammes.'

'I don't have that much cash on me,' Eamonn said hopefully.

'That's all right, buddy,' McNally said, his face twisting into a leer. 'I trust you, don't I?'

CHAPTER 10

The temperature had dropped a few notches and night was closing in as Danny walked Jazz to the precinct house. Though she was feeling bruised and miserable she insisted on going in; she needed to get the story on McNally – and his release. Her captain should be able to help.

Danny kissed her gently. Jazz smiled at him and disappeared inside. They'd decided to risk one more night in his apartment. No matter how good his connections were, McNally would never track them down that fast.

Danny hurried down Forty-second Street and Times Square. He was aware that darkness had become his greatest friend, wrapping him in its cloak of anonymity. In the gathering dusk he could be just another hustler, another pimp, another dealer, another curious tourist trying to hook into the seedy squalor of the Triple X-rated movies, the peep shows and the live girlie acts.

Danny thought how ironic it was that he had come to New York hoping to be picked out of the pack and put in the spotlight. Here he was now eagerly embracing the shadows.

He walked down the steps into Times Square subway, not so revolted this time by the smell of stale piss and vomit. Danny looked more considerately than before at the panhandlers and derelicts who used the place to shelter from the cold. The events of the past hours had made him realise that no one had absolute control over his or her own destiny.

He stood on the platform waiting for the subway. A young busker was playing classical violin nearby. He had a music stand in front of him and his violin case lay open at his feet. His reward was mostly in quarters, but Danny also noted a healthy number of dollar bills. He walked across and dropped fifty cents into the case. Solidarity with fellow musicians.

Night was fully in by the time Danny emerged into the cold wind at Astor Place. Eight blocks from home.

He felt like he was always eight blocks from home. He'd lost count of the number of record companies and publishers he called to over the past few weeks. Until today the best reaction he'd had was from a female A & R executive who'd told him his songs were 'cute'. Today though, after his encouraging meeting with Rick Dawdle, the eight blocks did not seem as formidable.

St Mark's Place was buzzing, as always. A guy came cycling towards him on the sidewalk.

'No brakes! No brakes!' he shouted indignantly. People scattered to get out of his way. Danny scanned his face as he passed. There wasn't a trace of humour. New York wasn't funny any more.

He hurried along, gazing hungrily in the windows of the restaurants and bars as he went by. If it's bad for me, Danny wondered, what must it be like for the penniless and the homeless?

At least he had his eggs. Because he was so broke, Danny had avoided eating out as much as possible. Instead he was surviving on a diet of pure eggs. 'One more fucking omelette and I'll start laying eggs myself,' he muttered aloud.

Danny closed his hand around the money in his jeans pocket and pulled it out to examine it. Jazz had bought lunch, so he still had the guts of the twenty dollars he had brought out with him. A slice of pizza would be a welcome change.

He pushed open the door of the pizza shop on First Avenue. The warm blast of air was such a welcome contrast to the stinging cold outside that he just stood for a minute soaking up the heat. He surveyed the menu on a lit-up board above the counter.

'A slice of pepperoni with mushroom, please.'

'Large, medium or small?' asked the nervy Italian behind the counter.

Here we go again, groaned Danny. America, the land of choices. Small, medium or large. White bread, brown or rye, pumpernickel, bap, French roll. Toasted or untoasted. Butter or Miracle Whip. Thousand Island, honey mustard, French, Italian, vinaigrette or house. Swiss, American, Californian Jack, cheddar or mozzarella. Coffee – caffeinated or decaff. Tea – iced, hot, regular or herbal. Coke – diet, diet-decaff, classic or regular. To go or eat here.

'Medium slice and small Coke to go, please.'

Danny took the boxed slice of pizza and stuck it inside his jacket. He could feel the heat next to his heart. He stuffed his Coke in his pocket, turned up his collar and headed back out to face the cold wind. Two more blocks to go and he would be home.

The wind was knifing its way up from the East River as Danny reached Sixth Street. Head down, he walked briskly down the street, past a building where scaffolding and a hoarding protruded a few feet on to the sidewalk. As he passed the doorway, a sudden movement made him look quickly into the shadows. A large black shape lurched out from the darkness.

Danny took off at a run. Shit! He had broken the rules he had established for himself: Always be aware of what is going on a block ahead of you and a block behind you. Always walk on the outside of the sidewalk. Avoid all doorways and scaffolding.

He stopped running and stared back up the street. The

large black shape resolved itself into a big black wino. Danny's heart thumped furiously as he realised that it could just as easily have been McNally lying in wait in the doorway.

He let himself into the apartment and put the chain-lock on the door. All the lights were off, except for the light on the cooker panel, so he knew that neither Gail nor Anton was home. Good. He didn't feel like having to talk to either of them. There was far too much going on in his head.

He flicked on the light in the kitchen and went through the letters on the countertop, knowing full well that there would be none for him.

He wondered how Mary was getting on, and the kids. Maybe it could all still work out if this deal were to come through and he could get his hands on a few dollars to take the pressure off. If he could just learn not to fuck about with other women.

The red light was flashing on the answering machine. He walked to the phone and pressed the replay button. He listened to two messages for Gail and one for Anton before he heard the familiar voice of his father.

'Danny, this is your Dad. It's seven o'clock in the evening my time and I'd like you to ring me urgently as soon as you get in. You can reverse the charges. Okay?'

His father sounded stiff and awkward talking to the machine, even so Danny could detect a note of real seriousness.

He picked up a magazine. The first thing he owed

himself was a leisurely visit to the can. He flicked up the bathroom light and saw the note propped on the wash-hand basin.

> Someone is leaving pubic hairs in the shower after use. This is very distasteful to the rest of us and we would be obliged if more care and attention could be paid to leaving the bathroom clean for others.

'Good old Gail, that fucking cow,' Danny said out loud. He knew 'someone' meant him even though he always left the bathroom spotless – except maybe for that morning when he had been in such a rush to get to his appointment. Oh well. He was having a relationship with Gail even though they never seemed to meet.

When he finished in the bathroom, Danny picked up the phone and dialled the operator to reverse the charges. He hated ringing his father. He had had to borrow money from him for his airfare and the price he had paid was yet another lecture about getting a steady job and forgetting about music.

'Hello, Dad. It's Danny.'

'Danny. How are you, son?'

'I'm fine, Dad. Fine.'

'Good, good.'

'Dad, what's the matter? You said it was urgent?'

'Well it is, son. Now before I say anything, let me tell

you that nobody is seriously hurt –'

'What are you talking about nobody seriously hurt?' Danny shouted, panic in his voice. 'What's happened? Is it Mary? The kids?'

'Mary had a bit of an accident in the car. She ran into a lamppost and she's in hospital, but they expect to let her out tomorrow and young Danny and Deirdre are okay. They just had cuts and bruises. I thought you'd want to know.'

'Jesus fucking Christ, of course I want to know.'

'Now, son, there's no need to go taking the Lord's name in vain.'

Danny held the phone away from his face and threw his eyes up to heaven. Stupid fucker, he mouthed silently.

'What about the car? Is the car wrecked?'

'No, the car isn't really any more wrecked than it was, but the front wheel on the left side is badly buckled and the radiator is punctured.'

'And where are the kids now?'

'They're with Mary's mother.'

'Have you been on to her?'

'I have.'

'Will Mary be going to her mother's tomorrow when she gets out of hospital?' At least he could call her there.

'She will, I think.'

'Listen, thanks for ringing me, Dad.'

'Okay, son. Is everything else going all right there? Have you enough money?'

'Yes, Dad, everything's fine.' Danny wondered what his father would say if he heard the truth.

'Because you know, Danny, if you want to come home, Johnny Duggan says you can start in his factory any time you like.'

'Thanks, Dad,' Danny said, trying to keep the exasperation out of his voice. 'Say hello to Mam and I'll ring you in a few days.'

Danny's mouth drew into a grim line. He did the only thing that made any sense, he made a cup of tea. Concentrating totally on the mechanics of making it, he closed his mind to everything until it was poured and ready. Then he sat at the table and let himself address all his problems.

Mary needed the car so it would have to be repaired. With McNally on his trail, he had had to pass up playing in My Wild Irish Rose, that had cost him a precious one hundred dollars. Maybe he should try getting a gig somewhere else, somewhere McNally wouldn't think of looking.

Danny rang information and got the number for Sin É. By all accounts it was the trendiest café in the East Village and he had heard good things about the place.

He got on to a guy called Peter Burke. Not only had he heard of Danny and Poison Pig but he'd just put down the phone from someone wondering whether a Danny Toner had been in.

'You're a popular guy,' Peter went on. 'There was a guy in here this morning looking for you as well.'

Danny gulped. The guy had been tall, darkish and asking

lots of official-type questions. From Immigration was Peter's guess.

'I told him I'd never heard of you,' said Peter.

'Thanks, mate,' Danny said relieved. 'And you won't let him know I was on?'

'Not a word.'

Danny walked back to the kitchen and put the kettle on for the second time. Things were hotting up. He turned and putting on his Clint Eastwood scowl, snarled at his reflection in the small mirror on the wall, 'Go ahead, make my tea.'

CHAPTER 11

The headlights were still following Jazz. This time she wasn't imagining it. Three times in the last twenty minutes she had thought she noticed a car moving very slowly behind her. She checked her gun, it was sitting snugly in the small shoulder holster. Casually she crossed the street, giving herself a chance to glance backwards. In the glare of the lights she couldn't see the occupants or even the make of car.

As she passed a doorway, a grizzled old derelict pulled the flap on his cardboard home a little tighter around him. A merciless wind was blowing in off the Hudson River, darting like a million small tornadoes into every crevice, swirling papers and dust into small upward spirals.

Jazz regretted her determination to work. She felt

bruised and aching and every step brought a fresh reminder of Vinny.

Tonight she felt different. No one had ever beaten her before. She was scared but she knew she would have to face Vinny tomorrow and remove her things from his apartment. And what about Danny? She had walked him into trouble and now Jack was under threat as well. McNally was really dangerous and she couldn't predict what the outcome might be. Everything was happening too fast.

She glanced over her shoulder. The headlights were still there. She felt her heartbeat quicken as she reached for her radio on the inside lapel of her jacket.

'Unit 24 to Central, my location is Fifty-first approaching Eleventh Avenue. I'm being trailed by what looks like a dark-coloured Sedan, behaving suspiciously. I can't see occupants ... request back-up car to investigate.'

The line crackled. 'Unit 24, car on way.'

'Ten-four.' Jazz forced herself to keep walking at an even pace. She had just reached the corner of Eleventh Avenue when she heard the sound of a siren in the distance. She walked a little quicker, keeping herself close in to the wall. She took a quick glance back.

The headlights took off, hurtling towards her. She flattened herself against the wall. A large maroon Sedan, tires squealing, went careering round the corner on two wheels. She could see what looked like two men in the front, but the car was travelling too fast for her to get a clear look at them. Sirens blaring, lights flashing, the patrol car came roaring up to the corner in pursuit. Jazz pointed up Eleventh Avenue, but already the patrol car had slid out on to the main thoroughfare after the Sedan.

Jazz's heart was palpitating wildly. She listened to the siren recede into the distance. Then she tucked her gun back in its holster and straightened her jacket. She could use a cup of coffee, but she'd better stick around until she knew the outcome of the chase.

Minutes later the patrol car swung back around the corner of Fifty-first and pulled in at the kerb. Jazz approached the open window on the driver's side.

'You Mahony?' asked the cop, sticking his head out of the window.

'Yeah.'

'Get in for a minute.' He nodded towards the back of the patrol car.

Jazz climbed into the back. She smiled to herself at the irony. So this was what it looked like for the ones who got busted, a cheesegrater view through the metal grille that separated her from the policemen in the front seat.

'They got away, huh?' Jazz asked.

'Not exactly.' The two cops exchanged looks.

'What d'you mean "not exactly".'

'We caught them and pulled 'em over, but it wasn't that simple.'

'Why? What's going on here? Who were they?'

The cop in the driver's seat turned round and looked at

Jazz, his face a mixture of suspicion and sympathy. 'They were Internal Affairs.'

'IAD!' The disbelief showed on Jazz's face.

'I'm sorry, Mahony, but that's what their IDs said.'

'Hold on.' Jazz was panicky now. 'Did they say why they were following me?'

'They said they didn't have to give a reason.'

'So you just let them go?'

'Hey, there was nothing else I could do.'

'Thanks a lot, pal.' Jazz was fuming as she pushed open the door and climbed back out on to the sidewalk. She slammed the door in temper and frustration.

'Go! Go on,' she said, waving the car away. 'Don't keep looking at me like that. I didn't do nothing wrong. So fuck you. Right?'

Jazz was worried now. How much did IAD know? And why were they following her? She hadn't done anything wrong. They only followed people who had done something wrong. Could they be using her as bait to get to McNally? Even worse, could they think that somehow she was mixed up with McNally?

CHAPTER 12

The door buzzer gave Danny a start. He got up from the table where he had been compiling a list of songs for his new money-making idea, busking, and crossed to the intercom.

'Yeah?'

'Danny, it's me, Jazz,' she hissed.

He pressed the release button for the front door and waited for her to come upstairs. When she saw him she made a weak attempt at a smile, but it didn't quite come off.

'Hello, Mrs Glum,' Danny said. 'You're finished early. Tough day at the office?'

This time she managed a smile. 'I'm sorry, Danny. I guess I'm a bit freaked.' She told him about being trailed and what the cops had said.

'Well, you've every right to be freaked,' said Danny, seating her at the table. 'You look like a woman who needs a good Irish remedy.'

'What's that?'

'A nice cup of tea.'

'D'you have coffee?'

'I can't stand a stroppy patient. You're having tea.'

'Okay,' she said meekly. 'Tea.'

Danny filled the kettle and flicked the switch on. He needed time to figure things out.

'Danny,' said Jazz slowly. 'There's more.'

Danny groaned inwardly.

'I went back to the precinct house. I had to find out more about the guys from IAD, you know, while they were still working tonight.'

'And?'

'McNally must have good connections – he was back on the street in hours. And apparently he went looking to see who fingered him. He checked on the records for last night and found out it was me that put the call in. One of the drug squad guys heard him saying that he was going after me and some Irish kid, because he thinks the two of us are in cahoots – is this making sense?'

'Yeah. I'm the stupid Irish kid. But where do the IAD come into it?'

'You're going to love this bit. They figured if they staked me out, they might catch McNally in the act. They've been watching this guy for a long time and they want him bad.'

'So they were prepared to let you be the bait?' Danny said outraged.

'Yeah. And one more thing, Danny.' She paused guiltily. 'They know you're an illegal, which means Immigration will be on your tail as well.'

Danny bit on his knuckle. 'Sweet Jesus, the drug squad, the IAD, Vinny and possibly Immigration. Who isn't looking for me?' If they knew he was illegal, his time was up. They would throw him out for sure. But if they wanted to catch McNally, they mightn't move until McNally tried something. Danny could risk the Paddy's Day gig at Jack's, so at least he'd have another hundred dollars and he might even hear something from Rick Dawdle.

'Danny, I'm really sorry.'

Danny turned to face her. He didn't know whether to be mad or not. But Jazz looked genuinely shook by her experience earlier. In for a penny, in for a pound, he thought.

'It's okay, Jazz, even though it's not okay – if you know what I mean.'

She smiled weakly.

'You must have been pretty scared out there.'

'I was. At first I thought it might be Vinny following me, but then when the car kept following me and not getting any closer, I started to worry.' She paused. She almost wished it had been Vinny. The way she was feeling tonight, she could have handled him no problem.

'You know what really pissed me off?' she continued.

'The guys in the patrol car. They were looking at me like I had done something real bad – you don't have any idea what bad news IAD is, Danny. It's the worst thing that can happen you if you're a cop. They're complete bastards. They get special pleasure out of busting one of their own and they have all these special powers, like not having to tell you why they're investigating. Pricks.'

'Tut, tut,' Danny said, wagging a finger. 'Language, Officer Ma*hony*.'

She laughed and reached over to him. 'Sorry! Give me a hug.'

'Hugs are dangerous,' Danny said, taking her on to his lap and wrapping his arms around her. 'Fucking is fun, but hugs are worms.'

The kettle sang out, and Danny extricated himself from the chair. He made the tea slowly and methodically and each time he looked up Jazz was staring at him. He remembered their love-making the night before. And he realised with resignation that once again he was a slave to his desire, and everything, including his family and his safety, was playing second fiddle to his standing cock.

'What are you staring at?' he asked.

'You,' she said.

'What's wrong with me?'

'Nothing,' she replied. 'That's the problem.'

'Don't be fooled by this good humour and handsome exterior,' Danny said. 'Inside I'm a mixture of Hannibal Lecter and Pee Wee Herman.'

Jazz laughed out loud.

Danny poured the tea and brought the two cups to the table. 'Thanks,' she said. 'You're really sweet.'

He lifted her back on to his lap again. She turned to face him and laid a hand on his cheek. Her lips parted as they found his and Danny slid his tongue into her mouth as far as it would go. He played his tongue under her upper lip. Slowly he traced the line of her lip. She pulled him to her tighter and then gasped as he sucked her full lip into his mouth.

He could feel himself go hard in anticipation. If this was going to be anything like the night before, he knew he was in for a hot time. He slid his hand inside her jacket but stopped abruptly as it came to rest on her shoulder holster.

He pulled away from her. 'Is that a gun in your pocket or are you just glad to see me?'

'That's my line, fool,' she laughed. 'Hold on and I'll just take it off.' She looked at him and saw the grin curling on the side of his mouth. 'Yes, asshole, that's what I'm thinking and you're going to love it.' She let her hand wander down on to his crotch.

'Hold everything!' Danny said. 'I think we'd better go into the bedroom. I dread to think what kind of note I'd get from my pal, Gail, if she found us fornicating in her front room.'

He led Jazz to the bedroom. Once inside she began to take off her clothes. She pulled her shirt up over her firm round breasts and Danny was horrified to see bruises and welts on her arms and ribs.

'Jesus Christ,' he said. 'I'd like to get that bastard and punch his fucking lights out.'

Jazz looked at the bruises on her arms. 'I thought I might have a few.' She slipped off her skirt and tights and stood before Danny in just her knickers. A huge purple bruise ran almost the length of her thigh. 'That's a beaut,' she said.

'You poor kid,' Danny said. 'Hey, listen, we don't have to do anything.'

'Let me be the judge of that,' she said. She hooked her thumbs into her knickers and slid them slowly to the ground.

Danny stood transfixed. He took her and laid her flat on the bed. She lifted his hand and guided it into the black triangle of hair. He felt her moistness and he put his lips to her navel. She sighed as his warm mouth moved down her body.

'How about a 68?' Danny said.

'What's that?' she murmured.

'I'll go down on you and you can owe me one.'

They lay in silence in the dark. Danny's hand still resting in between her legs, stroking her gently.

'So what would you have done if that had been Vinny following you tonight?'

'I don't know,' said Jazz. 'I really don't know. I was thinking about that on my way here in the cab. I mean I've been living with him for a year now, but I know very little about him.'

'How long did you know him before you moved in with him?'

''Bout six weeks. I met him at a bowling alley. I was there with a bunch of us from work and one of them knew him.'

'You must have got on with him pretty well?'

'Yeah, I did. It wasn't love but I was tired of being on my own. It's tough, y'know. So that's why I moved in with him.'

'Why did you have such a big fight last night?' Danny could sense her reluctance to tell. 'Okay. Look, I'm not complaining, and I don't need to know but can I ask one other question? Why did you have sex with me last night?'

She gulped at his frankness. 'I don't – I did – because I wanted to – that is, I mean, I liked you and it just kind of happened.' She saw the doubt in his eyes. 'Danny, I know what you're thinking, but I swear you're the first person I've slept with since I met Vinny. I promise you. I don't fool around.'

'Okay,' said Danny slowly. 'I believe you. It's just I'd hate to find myself between you and Vinny for no good reason. And he definitely never hit you before?'

'I swear on my mother's grave.'

'Okay, okay.' This time he laughed. 'I'm sorry if I'm a bit paranoid. It's been a hell of a few hours.'

'I know,' she said. 'I know.'

Danny reached over her and switched the light off. 'Are

you going to help me with my busking extravaganza tomorrow?'

'What's busking?' asked Jazz.

'You don't know?' he said incredulously. 'You know, singing in the subway or on the street.'

'Oh yeah, I get it.' She smiled. 'But what's all this about?'

'Oh shit,' Danny said. 'I forgot to tell you. I got a call from my dad to tell me that my wife and the kids had an accident in the car. Luckily nobody's hurt, but the car is going to cost money, so I have to get my hands on some dollars as quick as I can. I'm going to ring Jack and tell him I'm doing St Paddy's Day regardless of McNally and tomorrow I'm going busking.'

'So where are you busking?'

'Well, depends on the weather, but I thought I'd start in Times Square subway, where the shuttle from Grand Central comes in. And if that turns out to be a crock, I was thinking of going down to Washington Square Park to try and catch some of the lunchtime crowd and the tourists.'

'You're crazy, but I'm off work for the next few days. My captain told me to lie low, so I can come along and keep an eye on you.'

She moved closer to him and stroked his back. 'Do you remember that 68 you gave me and you said I could owe you one?' she asked.

'Yeah.'

'Well, mister, it's payback time.'

CHAPTER 13

Jack dragged the plastic sack out across the hall and dropped it into the rubbish chute. He walked back into his apartment and surveyed his day's work. The apartment was as clean as it had been the first time he walked into it.

Mentally he thanked McNally. His rude intrusion into Jack's life had, in the space of a few hours, brought about a great change. For the first time in years Jack felt truly alive, his brain sharp, his reflexes finely tuned. McNally's taunts were like a red rag to a bull and the singlemindedness that had preserved Jack's sanity in his time in prison had clicked into action again almost instantly. The tidiness of the apartment was better than a hit of alcohol. It spoke to him and it said 'control'.

He studied himself in the small mirror just inside his front door. The face that looked back at him was jowled and raddled from the booze. Jack knew he looked a lot more than his thirty-eight years, but in his fresh shirt and his good suit, he looked crisper than he had for many a long day.

The phone rang. He picked up the receiver but didn't speak until he heard Danny's voice.

'Jack. How are you doing? How's your lip?'

'A bit sore, but I'm a tough man,' he laughed. 'What's up?'

'Well, there's a lot more shit going on. Jazz is being followed by the Internal Affairs because those bastards are hoping McNally will have a crack at her. They're using her as bait.'

'McNally knows about Jazz?'

'Yeah. This scumbag seems to have no trouble getting information.'

'You're dead right.' Jack was wondering just who his informants were.

'Anyway, Jack, I just wanted to ask if you had got anybody else yet for St Paddy's Day?'

'As a matter of fact, I haven't. Everybody seems to be booked up.'

'Well, put me back in, Jack. I need the dough badly and with the list of people who are keeping an eye on McNally, I don't think he'll try anything. Anyway, you told him I wasn't playing until next week.'

Jack was about to offer words of caution, but he checked himself. He would look out for Danny. He would be his protector. If McNally came around, he'd have him to deal with before he could get to Danny. 'Okay, Danny. We'll just have to be careful, that's all.'

Jack replaced the receiver and looked at his watch. He had twenty minutes before he had to meet Eamonn Doherty.

He walked quickly to his bedroom and reached down and opened the drawer in the locker beside his bed. He searched under the piles of clothes and lifted out the Walther PPK revolver. He hesitated as he looked at it lying flat on his palm and then, as though he had overruled his own objection, he checked the magazine and stuck the gun into the waistband of his trousers. He buttoned up his jacket, switched off the bedside light and walked to the front door. He took one last look at his cleaning handiwork and closed the door behind himself.

Jack pushed the door of My Wild Irish Rose open and saw Eamonn sitting at the end of the bar, drinking a beer. He clapped him on the back. 'How are you doing?'

'Rightly, thanks.'

'Deirdre!' he called. 'Get us another beer and a soda for me.'

'A soda?' she looked at him as if he'd gone mad.

'No jokes, Deirdre,' he said, smiling. 'Just a soda.'

'Off the drink?' Eamonn asked.

Jack hesitated for a moment. 'Yeah, I suppose you could say that.'

He looked Eamonn straight in the eye. 'So look at you. You were only a kid the last time I saw you.'

'Yeah, I suppose I was. I came here as soon as I could get away from Belfast though.'

'You were never tempted to follow the brothers into the Provos?'

'Not even for a minute. Don't ask me why. It was never an option for me, even though John and Michael and myself were so close, and, of course, me ma and da never let us forget the struggle.'

'Did you get a shock when you saw me?' Eamonn took in Jack's puffy face and his slack belly. This was a very different guy from the Kevin O'Toole who'd stood between his brother and a bullet.

He nodded. 'That's putting it mildly,' he said. 'I knew you'd skipped to America, but apart from hearing rumours that you were in New York, I knew nothing.'

'Yeah, I'm a long time here now. It's funny, I heard your name several times but I never suspected it might be you. I mean you really were young the last time I saw you and I wasn't getting a lot of information from home. I was too terrified that I might be caught, so I've kept very much to meself. Trust nobody, that's my motto. 'Specially people from Belfast.'

'Does that include me?' Eamonn asked cautiously.

'I suppose it would have to, but that's one of the things I wanted to talk to you about.'

'Okay,' Eamonn said. 'Let me put my cards on the table.

I'd prefer that I didn't know what I know about you, but you did save Michael's life once, and that's worth something.' It was worth a lot, but Eamonn didn't want anyone from those bad old days, even Jack, having a claim on him. 'I don't have any truck with anyone political here and I stay away from Irish functions as much as I can, so the chances of me passing information are none and fuck all.'

'Fair enough,' Jack said. Michael's brother would never lie to him, he knew that.

'And I don't want to know what you're doing now either, if it's all the same to you, the less I know, the better.'

'I think what you're trying to find out is, am I still in?' Jack said. 'Well, I'm not. When I got here first, I found it very frustrating that I couldn't be involved, organising money and guns and whatever, but the longer I was away from it, the more I realised that you couldn't bomb your way to a United Ireland. It wasn't achieving anything. It'd probably have helped the cause if I'd been busted, like Joe Doherty. Having someone in jail and in and out of court here helped to keep the story on the political agenda, but I told them I wasn't interested in becoming a martyr and eventually they had to accept it.'

Eamonn listened without taking his eyes from Jack. 'I'm glad,' he said. 'It makes it easier for us to be friends. Does Danny know anything?'

'He doesn't,' Jack said. 'I think it's better that way. He has enough to worry about as it is.'

Eamonn sighed and thought of McNally. 'You're too right.'

'So tell me about this boy McNally?'

'He's a wicked fucker. He told me he paid you a visit. Is that where you got your split lip?'

'Yeah,' replied Jack, fingering the cut.

'McNally's a dangerous bastard. He's wild keen to get his hands on Danny Toner. Says he's going to kill him.'

'D'you believe him?'

'I honest to fuck don't know. I think he knows you're lying to him, but he's just turning up the heat on everyone. He told me that I'd better help him find Danny or he'd get some of his heavies to start fights up in our bar.'

'So how did you get involved with him?'

'He was just there one night and when someone suggested a bit of coke, he was the man who came up with it. He's been hanging 'round ever since.'

'Did you know he was a cop?'

'Sure I did, but I didn't give a shite if he was the Pope, as long as he had the coke.'

'You're a terrible man to be sniffing away good money on that stuff.'

'Yeah. Yeah. You don't have to tell me. Look, McNally told me today that he'll be hitting me for two grammes a week, whether I want it or not.'

'That's heavy all right. But I hope it doesn't mean you're going to hand him Danny.'

Eamonn shifted uncomfortably in his seat. He was

prepared to do a lot to keep McNally off his back – and keep The Buzz running smoothly.

'Look, Eamonn,' Jack went on, 'Danny's a friend of mine. I don't want to see him hurt. Leave McNally to me. I'll sort him out. How much does McNally know about me?'

'To tell you the truth, I haven't a clue.'

'Well, if this shit goes any further,' said Jack, 'I could find myself out on Riker's Island in a cell, waiting to be shipped back to Crumlin Road.'

'Don't I know it. I tried to put him off as much as I could about you, but he's such a thick gobshite that he could do anything. Does anybody else here know who you are?'

'Only the guy who set me up here with my new identity, but I haven't spoken to him for four years now. He knows where I work and where I live. Is McNally political at all? Would he have any contact with the Provos?'

'He mouths off from time to time, but like a lot of them he hasn't a fucking clue what he's talking about. So what do you want to do about it?'

Jack was silent for a moment. If McNally got wind that Danny was playing on St Patrick's Day, anything could happen.

'Can I ask you the truth?' Eamonn said. 'Did Danny finger McNally?'

'Danny was as surprised as you were by the bust,' Jack answered. 'The girl with him, Jazz, she's a cop, works for the Anti-Crime squad. She recognised McNally and tipped the drug boys at the DEA.'

Eamonn nodded, remembering how Jazz had reappeared after the bust. 'And where does she fit into all this now? McNally didn't mention her.'

'No? Well, he's after her too. He thinks Danny and her were in it together. The IAD are after McNally too and are using Jazz as bait. And, I haven't said this to him, but I'll bet the reason Danny hasn't been picked up yet is because he's being used too.'

'Fuck me, it's a right nest of worms,' Eamonn said, gulping back the last of his drink.

'Yeah, you're right. Will you have another beer?'

'I will.'

Jack signalled to Deirdre down the bar for another round.

'D'you know something?' Eamonn said.

'What?'

'Me Belfast accent hasn't been this thick for years.'

CHAPTER 14

Jazz could see Danny looking at his watch. It was only just after eleven-thirty in the morning and she was barely late. But he was standing under the arch in Washington Square Park, scanning Fifth Avenue anxiously.

She laughed when she saw him. He was dressed in a leopardskin baseball cap, a multi-coloured T-shirt over several layers of jumpers, a pair of imitation leather trousers and on his feet were those odd brown brogues. A pair of sunglasses rounded off the colourful outfit.

Danny saw her and began to make his way towards her. He walked between two parked cars and suddenly crouched down as if he was tying his laces. She saw him whip out the remains of a joint, light it, and inhale it deeply all in one smooth movement. The guy was an expert. Then he stood up and exhaled a white-blue cloud as he walked.

'Hey, Irish. What's happening?'

'The way we're dressed, we should be on our way to Bellevue Mental Hospital,' Danny giggled. 'That's what's happening.'

Jazz looked down at her own clothes and smiled. She was wearing her standard leather biker's jacket and calf-length boots, black leggings and a yellow-and-black polka dot top and, on her one corkscrew curl of hair, she had tied an extravagant red ribbon.

'You're right,' she said, laughing. 'We look like an accident in a Thrift Shop. How did you get on in Times Square?'

'The crowd reacted with great indifference and a little hostility thrown in for good measure, which got me dander up, so I'm ready again.'

'And well stoned too.' She grinned.

'Is the Pope a Catholic?' he asked and laughed back. 'And what about you? Did you have any luck finding us a hideaway?'

'Temporarily. I called this friend of mine, Ice –'

'Ice? Her name is *Ice?*'

'Yeah. She's a stripper, but she's real nice. You'll like her. She's going out of town tonight for a week, so we can stay in her place till she gets back. It gives me a chance to get my stuff from Vinny's.'

They started to walk into Washington Square, Danny's guitar banging into Jazz's leg.

'What's the story on Vinny? Did you talk to him?' he asked.

'I rang him this morning and he was like a little child, begging me to go back and all that, saying it would never happen again.' It would have been difficult for her to be so firm with Vinny if Danny hadn't been around, she thought. He gave her something to compare Vinny with.

Danny put his arm around her. 'And how do you feel about that?'

'I feel nothing. Cold, that's how I feel. Anyway, it's all bullshit. It's only his pride that's bothering him, more of that Italian macho shit.'

'Did my name come up?'

'Yeah, but I told him you were none of his business.'

Danny sighed. 'Jazz, it would've been easier to say I wasn't around any longer.'

'Yeah, I know,' she said angrily. 'But screw him. It *is* none of his goddamn business. It's my life.' She stopped walking. Suddenly it seemed very cold.

'And is he going to let you take your things out without bothering you, because if you want to, I'll go with you.' Danny was surprised to hear himself make the offer. Perhaps he wanted an excuse to tear into Vinny.

'Thanks, Danny, but I don't think that'd be a good idea. He'll do a lot of bullying and shit and I'll tell him I'll think about it and then it'll be all over, once I get my things out.'

'But you're going to need a car to move your stuff.'

'Nah. I'll just take a cab.'

'Jack'd do it. I know he would. He likes you. I'll give him a call later and fix it up.'

How much will he like me if McNally beats him up again, Jazz wondered. Still, she did feel that Jack liked her and if he was generous enough to help, she'd be happy to know that he was there. Jack was the sort of person you felt glad to have as a friend. In the meantime, she must try and make sure nothing happened to Danny.

'So are you all ready for your stay at Ice's place?'

'Yeah. I just have to throw a few things in a bag.' He paused. 'Will I need a posing pouch?' he asked.

'Of course, and some oil to rub into those big muscles of yours,' she said, smiling. 'I'll tell you what.'

'What?'

'You bring the muscles. I'll bring the oil.'

CHAPTER 15

Jack took a long hot shower, then turned the water to cold for a wake-up blast. It had been a long time since he had woken without the bilious furry taste of drink in his mouth and a dullness in his head. He dried himself as he walked through to the sittingroom.

On the coffee table he had assembled every scrap of paper in the apartment, bills, letters, permits, receipts, anything addressed to, or signed by, Jack Killoran.

Alongside the paperwork were two piles of stacked photographs. The first contained photographs of Jack with friends and entertainers in My Wild Irish Rose. The second, and much smaller, pile showed Jack with two different women, the only reminders that remained of his attempts to find a partner in New York. But Jack had too many secrets to be able to share his life.

When he had finished drying himself, he dressed quickly in a crisp shirt, a muted green tie and his good grey suit. He stood in front of the mirror, tugged his tie into position and felt satisfied that he looked suitably anonymous.

He picked up the pile of documents and carried them to the sink in the kitchen. He flicked a lighter into flame and holding the various bits of paper over the sink, burnt them one by one and washed the black residue down the drain. If Immigration was going to search his apartment and he had to make a run out of New York, he would make sure that they would find nothing that would be useful in tracking him down.

He picked up the photographs, turning them upside down to avoid looking at them as he burnt them. When he came to the last photograph, however, he turned it over. It was a black and white snapshot of himself and four other men. He studied it, gave a rueful shake of his head and stuck it into his inside pocket.

Next to the photographs lay his gun. He picked it up and tucked it in the waistband of his trousers. His Nike training bag was filled with just enough clothes to make the bag comfortable and unobtrusive to carry. Casting a cold glance round the room, Jack strode out and locked the door behind him. Maybe he was being alarmist, he thought, maybe his cover hadn't been blown. But he couldn't afford to take any chances.

As soon as Jack emerged on to the street the hairs on the back of his neck began to tingle. He stood and sniffed at the air as though he was enjoying the piquant bouquet of gasoline and other street fumes. Slowly he let his eye travel down the line of cars opposite. Someone was watching him.

Jack strolled casually down Twenty-eighth Street with the air of a man who had all the time in the world. He marvelled at the way his street senses were coming back to him so quickly. He crossed to the far sidewalk and looked slowly back over his shoulder. He could see them following him, two men, one on foot and one in a blue Chevy. He smiled to himself. Looked like he was being tailed as well. He knew how to lead them a bit of a dance.

A couple of early drinkers sat along the bar of My Wild Irish Rose when Jack walked in. He called Deirdre down to the end of the bar. 'Anybody been in looking for me?' he asked in a low voice.

'No,' she replied, 'but two men were in inquiring about Danny Toner.'

'What were they like?'

'Suits.'

Jack walked quickly to the window. Carefully, so his trackers would not see him, he scanned the street. On the far side of Second Avenue, he could see the two men standing in a doorway, and doubleparked just ahead of them was the car that had followed him.

'Deirdre, I have a favour to ask.'

'Ask away.'

'The two guys who were in earlier, they followed me

here. I think they're from Immigration and I think they're after Danny. I'm going to duck out the back way, so if they come in, will you stall them for as long as you can?'

'No problem,' she said. 'But be careful, Jack.'

He squeezed her hand in gratitude and felt an answering pressure. If all this worked out, he thought ...

He stopped himself. Get a grip, man, a voice in his head said. This isn't a TV soap where hero gets girl, this is real life.

He slipped out through the back door into the small yard at the rear. He scaled the wall to the yard next door and repeated the process until he was almost at the end of the block. Stealthily he opened the gate into the lane and peered carefully up and down. He emerged into the lane and hurried to the street corner, where again he surveyed the scene carefully before he took off at a run. He ran until he came out, puffing hard, just above where his car was parked.

He gunned his car into life and headed for the The Buzz. His head was really clear now and he found himself enjoying the dice with cabs, cars and buses as he raced madly up the potholed and cracked roadway.

A block short of The Buzz he found a parking spot. He congratulated himself for stumbling on such a rarity and strode into the bar with a smile.

Inside, Eamonn was seated at the first table. They exchanged greetings, then there was a pause.

Jack hesitated. For a man used to being independent

this was difficult. He swallowed and then looked straight at Eamonn. 'I need a place to stay for a couple of days,' he said. 'The Immigration boys are on to Danny and I'm afraid if I stay in the line of fire, they might rumble me too.'

Eamonn looked hard at Jack. What did he owe him? Jack was a fugitive and if he was found in his apartment, Eamonn could be jailed for harbouring him. He would probably lose his Green Card as well. He wanted to say no, but he baulked at the thought of Jack being sent back to British justice.

'Okay,' he said resignedly. 'But only for a few days, d'you understand?' He realised with irony that he was about to imitate his father at last by providing a 'safe house' for one of the 'boys' on the run. That would have made his da proud. For the first time he understood how easy it would have been to submit to patriotic blackmail if he had stayed in Belfast.

'I promise that's all it'll be,' Jack said. 'You're a star, Eamonn.'

'D'you mind my asking, Jack, why you couldn't go to your handler here in New York?' Surely his handler could help him disappear again.

'Because I was serious when I told you I'd left all that behind. I don't want to get sucked into that again.'

Eamonn nodded. 'I can understand that. Well, d'you want to go to my place now?'

'I wouldn't mind a sandwich first.'

They ate, mostly in silence. They had almost finished

lunch when the door burst open and on a tide of rough laughter, McNally and two tough-looking guys came through the door.

'Hey!' McNally shouted, as soon as he saw them. 'What've we here? A romantic lunch for two?' He punched Jack on the shoulder. 'Does your faggoty singing friend know you're cheating on him?'

Jack gave McNally the same unyielding stare he had offered when he had been beaten in his apartment.

McNally couldn't hold eye contact, shifting his focus to Eamonn instead. 'You got my money?' he snarled.

'I just have to go and do a bit of business, but I'll be right back and I'll fix you up then.' Eamonn stood up.

'Yeah, sure. And while you're gone, me and the boys will have a little lunch – on you.' The goons laughed and sat down to Eamonn's unfinished lunch.

'C'mon, Jack, we'd better go,' said Eamonn.

Jack got up and they both walked to the door. Jack looked back over his shoulder. 'You've got your hands full there all right.'

CHAPTER 16

Jazz giggled as Danny pulled a woollen mitten from his pocket and hooked it onto the jagged ends of the guitar strings at the point where they wrapped around the pegs.

'Pretty fancy money bag, isn't it?' he said to Jazz.

She watched as Danny set up inside the Fifth Avenue entrance to Washington Square Park, underneath the big arch. The sun was at its warmest now and people were sitting down or strolling, even though they still had their heavy overcoats on.

One side of the square led into Greenwich Village, another into Lower Broadway, another into Eighth Street. And in the middle of all the ordinary people there was the usual collection of deadbeats – junkies, hippies, winos, guys playing frisbee, women walking dogs, a man with a snake around his neck, a guy selling hot dogs.

Danny pushed back his shoulders, took a deep breath and burst into song.

I've been a wild rover ...

He was amazed when a few punters actually stopped to listen. Give generously, folks, he willed them.

The first coin tumbled into his mitt – a quarter. It seemed to do the trick. Quarters began to flow.

Danny preened himself. Excuse me, I'm about to appear in a Japanese video.

A woman walking towards him took a sharp right and collided with a pram.

Danny grimaced. Jaysus, I can't be that bad, he thought. Maybe it was the suddenness of it.

They were paying attention now. Fourteen, fifteen, sixteen punters stopped in their tracks. Sure this was like a bleedin' concert.

I went into an alehouse ...

Another video and two photographs as well. Where would it all end? A headline in the *New York Times* 'The luck of the Irish – street singer signs million dollar deal'?

No, never, no more ...

Danny finished the song and bowed to the applause. As he lifted his head he noticed two men in suits staring at him. He looked around for Jazz. Where was she? He called out her name and she appeared beside him instantly.

'What's the matter?'

'Don't look around,' whispered Danny out of the corner of his mouth, 'but there are two guys in suits lounging near the tree, back behind you. They've been there since I started and they don't look comfortable.'

'Okay. I'll check 'em out.'

Shit, he thought, it was going to be hard to concentrate now with those two fuckers. Maybe they were Jazz's tail from the IAD. Better sing, he told himself. The punters were beginning to drift off.

> Well, here I am from Paddy's land
> A land of high renown ...

Now, what's this space cadet up to? he wondered.

'Hey, my friend. Hey man, you're pretty good. We like you.' A young wino with a bottle in a brown paper bag was dancing in front of Danny as he sang. With him were two scruffy-looking hippies, a large American Indian, two Rastafarians and a completely bald black man in a clerical collar, a Bible clutched in his hand.

Jazz, what the fuck! Danny could hardly believe his eyes. Oh Jesus, no. Jazz was confronting the two guys in suits.

'It's those two creeps from IAD,' Jazz said, coming up beside him again. 'I made the bastards show me their IDs. I'm sure you'll be thrilled to know the taller dickhead is

Irish, O'Malley, and the other jerk is a Polack, Yoblonski or something.'

'And I gather they're enjoying the show?'

'They don't seem eager to go.'

'That's just great. It means we're stuck with them permanently.'

'Unless we can find a way to lose them.'

'Easier said than done.' Danny looked up. 'Aw shit, my crowd just lost interest. Hold on till I get my cap and we'll go sit down and have a think about this.'

Danny picked up his cap which was heavy with money. 'Maybe we can buy them off,' he grinned.

'Bump them off,' put in Jazz. 'That'd suit me better.'

'Hey, man, are you going to sing again?' Danny turned to see the wino with the brown bag. He looked about thirty-five. He had a stubbly beard, liquid brown Jesus eyes and he was wearing a tattered old overcoat. Inside his bag was a pint of cheap whiskey, which he offered to Danny.

'No thanks,' Danny said. 'No offence, but I don't drink whiskey. You don't have a bottle of vodka, do you?'

The wino laughed. 'No, man, I sure don't. Hey, my name is Frank. You were pretty good there. You should stick around. They like you. You pulled a big crowd.'

'Thanks for the compliment, Frank. I'll do that.'

Danny put his arm around Jazz and walked her to a bench. They sat down, checking to see if they were still being watched.

'D'you think they know who I am?' Danny asked.

'I'm pretty sure.'

'Would they be likely to call in and tell the Immigration guys?'

'No way. These guys only care about themselves. They don't give a shit about other departments' problems.'

'What we need is a crowd and plenty of distraction. That way you could escape and I could join you later in Ice's. Write her address down for me while I go talk to Frank.'

Jazz wrote the address and watched as Danny went across to Frank. They talked animatedly and she saw Danny slip him something. They exchanged a handshake and then Danny walked up to her.

'In return for a few dollars, Frank and the Wino Tabernacle Choir are going to join me. We should be able to get enough people to create enough noise and confusion for you to slip off down to Ice's.'

'What about you?'

'I think you're their first concern, so they'll probably leg it after you. I'm going to waltz Frank and the boys over towards the Village and then, I'm going to make a run for it as well.'

'Let's do it.'

Danny got up and walked over to Frank and his gang. 'Okay, Frank. Here we go.'

Danny began to wiggle his hips and sing like Elvis. Frank and the other winos gathered in a half-circle in front of him and began to whoop and holler. A large crowd quickly gathered.

Danny egged the others on. The tall bald guy with the Bible was wiggling like a madman. The crowd started to laugh, intrigued by the antics of Frank and his wino friends. Danny took a quick look around, spotted the two IAD guys and nodded to Jazz. The timing was perfect. She took off at a run and with that Danny waltzed Frank and his friends across the path of the two men in suits.

They can't see. Go. Go! he urged silently. Good girl, that's it, run, run! From where he was standing, Danny watched the two guys legging it down Lower Broadway. Jazz had gone the other way.

Schmucks! crowed Danny. Time to take a bow and scram. Shit, he thought, if I stuck around to collect, I'd make a bundle. That's show biz, I suppose.

He slung his guitar on to his back and took off, running into Greenwich Village. 'Thanks, Frank,' he called over his shoulder.

'*Adios, amigo!*' Frank shouted back, before he turned and bowed extravagantly to a bemused crowd of people surrounding a handful of New York bums enjoying their fifteen seconds of fame.

CHAPTER 17

Danny glanced through the back window of the cab as they sped down Seventh Street. He was satisfied that no one was following him. He ripped off his lurid T-shirt and leopardskin cap. He would look less conspicuous in his shirt and trousers.

The cab pulled in at the corner and Danny paid off the driver. He peered carefully around the corner of Avenue B and when he saw it was clear, he hurried to the corner. In a quick burst he ran across the street and in the door of his apartment hallway.

The first thing that caught his eye as he entered the apartment was a note on top of the cooker.

> The pots and pans in this house have to be used by everyone. It would be polite to remove all egg stains after use.
>
> Thank you

Danny smiled. At least she hadn't missed her sunglasses.

He tore up Gail's note and went to his bedroom. With quick deliberate movements he pulled out his travel bag and packed his small pouch of grass, followed by his green shirt and green jeans. He would need those for St Patrick's Day, especially the dope.

He slipped off his leather trousers and shirt, took a quick shower and put on clean boxers, his black shirt and black jeans. He threw four pairs of socks, two shirts and some more clean shorts into the bag and zipped it up. He carried his bag and his leather jacket and left them down beside the phone.

He wasn't looking forward to his next move, but he knew he must ring Mary. He dialled the number and recognised her voice immediately.

'Mary. Hello. It's Danny.'

No response.

'How are you? It's Danny.'

'Fine.'

'That's good. My dad rang me and told me what happened.'

No response again.

'How are the kids?'

'Fine.'

'Nobody hurt too badly?'

'No.'

'Is the car gone in for repairs?'

'It's going in today.'

'I'll be able to wire some money on Monday, so you should be okay.'

'Fine.'

Danny became exasperated. 'For fuck's sake, Mary. Give me a break. I'm only ringing because I'm worried about you.'

There was still no response. Danny was boiling with rage, but he had to admit to himself that he'd guessed she might react like that. Besides, here he was having wild sex with Jazz and once again not being straight with her.

''Bye. I'll talk to you soon.'

He waited for a response but it didn't come, so he put down the phone.

Son of a bitch, what the fuck can you do? He felt like smashing something.

He took the remains of his cup of tea and placed the mug right outside Gail's door in the hope that she might kick it over.

He locked the apartment door behind him and walked down to the street. Once more he took a cautious look around before stepping outside. It was not a good time of the day for taxis, but he remembered the aphorism he had coined himself one night after too many drinks – a cab is like death, if you hang around long enough, yours will eventually come.

After five anxious minutes, a cab did pull in. As it drove away from the kerb, the driver leaned his head back and spoke over his shoulder in a thick middle-European accent. 'How are you today, sir?'

'Fine, thanks.' Screw this. The last thing he wanted was a chatty driver.

'You are a musician, sir?'

'Yes, I am.' What did his guitar case look like – a fucking golf bag?

'I, too, am a musician.'

'Really?' So that gave him the right to bore the arse off his passengers?

'I play the accordion, sir.'

'That's great.' Could he come home and chop it up for him?

'So what kind of music do you play?'

'A bit of rock. And some Irish folk music.' Unless of course he was playing Bulgarian accordion solos on guitar.

'Ah, Irish. The Chieftains. I like them. You know the Chieftains?'

'Yes. I know who they are.' Why pick on the Chieftains, the bastard.

'You are Irish too, sir?'

'Yeah.' Danny looked out the window impatiently. Maybe he should walk.

'Do you get a lot of girls playing music?'

'Girls?' Now what?

'I get lots of girls when I play music.'

'Is that so?' With that big ugly head?

'You ever fuck a black girl?'

'No.' What was going on here?

'You ever fuck a Chinese girl?'

'No.'

'You ever fuck a South American girl?'

Danny leaned forward until he could read the driver's identity plate. 'Drago, do you mind if I ask you a question?'

'No, sir, I do not mind.'

'Are you married?'

He looked back over his shoulder and flashed Danny a beaming smile. 'Oh yes, sir. But my dick is not.'

Danny couldn't help smiling. Guilt wasn't necessary. All you had to do was treat your penis as a separate person. There's not much difference between me and Drago, he mused.

'Here we are, sir. Thirty-Fourth Street.'

Danny climbed out and stood at the cab window. He paid his fare and tipped a dollar.

'One thing before you go, Drago.'

'Yes, sir?'

'You ever fuck an Irish girl?'

'No, sir. I did not.'

'Tough shit, Drago,' Danny gloated, as he turned on his heel. 'If you haven't fucked an Irish girl, you haven't lived.'

CHAPTER 18

Eamonn settled Jack into his apartment and showed him where everything was. Then he drove back towards The Buzz through the traffic, running his hand agitatedly through his hair. He hoped McNally would be gone. He was short of cash and he would have to take the two hundred dollars from the lunchtime takings to pay him. He knew there was no escape from telling Robbie what was going on. But should he tell him about Jack? They had tried to run the business without any secrets between them and now, as well as threatening Jack, Danny and Jazz, McNally was jeopardising their business relationship.

Eamonn nosed the car into a parking spot. He hated this time of evening, when twilight daubed everything with its murky brush. He pulled his coat tight against the cold wind and hurried through the gloom to The Buzz.

As he pushed open the door, he could hear McNally's loud guffaw. He noted, thankfully, that there were no other customers in the place.

'Hey you! C'mon over here and join the party!' McNally roared.

'Give me two minutes,' Eamonn said, breezing past. He joined Robbie at a table at the back of the bar.

'Jesus, I'm really sorry about that fucking moron.'

'Don't talk to me,' Robbie said, throwing his eyes to the ceiling. 'What's up?'

Eamonn took a deep breath, it was now or never. He told Robbie the whole story. McNally would have to be paid before he would leave the restaurant – or else. And the two goons were there as a guarantee that he meant what he said.

He looked up for a response. Robbie was looking at him with a mixture of anger and contempt. 'I'll lend you the money personally,' Robbie said stiffly, pulling out his wallet.

He counted out two hundred dollars and handed it to Eamonn, his face a mask of controlled fury. 'I don't need to ask the obvious, do I?'

'No, you don't,' Eamonn said quietly. 'I swear, Robbie, I haven't touched the restaurant money.'

Robbie just nodded grimly.

'Thanks,' said Eamonn. 'I'll sort this out, I promise.'

'You'd better.'

Eamonn walked to McNally's table, stuffing the money into his breast pocket on the way.

'Hey, make room for the *boss*,' McNally hooted. Eamonn could see he was pretty drunk, as were his two friends. 'We had a real special lunch, didn't we, boys?'

'Was there any food involved?' Eamonn asked wryly.

'Did you hear that, fellas? The harp is a fucking comedian. A sharp harp. Hey you!' he bellowed at the waitress, 'gimme a beer for Mr Sharp Harp here.'

'There's your money,' Eamonn said, flinging the two hundred dollars on the table.

'What a good boy you are,' McNally jeered. 'Want to go powder your nose now?' He threw two small packages of coke on to the table.

Eamonn shook his head.

'Oh, the poor boy's not in a party mood. We'll have to come by again tomorrow for St Paddy's Day. Maybe we'll see your faggoty friend, Danny Boy. Is he singing tomorrow?'

'I think he's singing up in the Bronx,' Eamonn lied.

'Is that right now? Well, you tell him that I'm real anxious to talk to him.' He began to sing. 'Oh Danny Boy, I'll blow your fucking head off.'

He howled with laughter at his own joke. Then he stopped and stared at Eamonn. 'You're not laughing at my new song.'

Eamonn stood up. 'You'll have to excuse me, I have a bit of business to catch up on.'

'You do that. And don't forget, tell Danny Boy we'll see him tomorrow.'

In the office at the back of the bar Robbie was sitting at the computer looking at stock inventory lists. He spoke without looking up. 'Your friend is still with us.'

Eamonn stood awkwardly by the door. 'Robbie, I got myself into this, and I'll get myself out of it, but I, well, I might need your support over the next few days.'

Robbie swivelled his chair round to face Eamonn. 'There's more, isn't there?'

'A bit,' Eamonn said grimly. 'Jack Killoran, you know the guy who was here with Danny the other night ...'

'What about him?'

'His real name isn't Jack Killoran. I won't tell you his real name because it's probably better if you don't know it, but he escaped from Crumlin Road ten years ago and he's been living here in New York for a few years now.'

Robbie looked at him, wondering what piece of startling news he would hear next. 'Does he fit into this McNally thing as well?'

'Yeah, but only because McNally beat him up and he likes Danny and doesn't want to see him get hurt. As it is, it looks like Danny will get thrown out by the Immigration guys anyway and because they're sniffing around, Jack thinks his real name will be discovered and they'll do him.'

'Is that why you had lunch with him?'

'He came to see me to ask me if he could stay in my place for a few days.'

'And you said *yes*?' Robbie couldn't believe his ears.

'What else could I do, Robbie? What would you have done? A guy comes to you and says, there's a good chance that I'll be caught and sent back to the Brits. Would you turn him in?'

Robbie pursed his lips and thought. 'No, I probably wouldn't. But Jesus, Eamonn, you're taking a terrible chance with your own personal life – and the business as well.'

'I know,' said Eamonn shamefacedly. 'That's why I wanted you to know everything. I screwed up big time. Dope and drink, fucks you up every time.'

CHAPTER 19

Jazz was sitting on the window ledge watching out for Danny when the cab pulled up. She watched him get out and talk to the driver and she thought how handsome he looked.

'He's here!'

Ice got to the window just as Danny entered the building. 'Shit! Missed him! This guy better live up to his billing after all I've heard about him.'

'He will,' Jazz said. 'And don't you go making those goo-goo eyes at him.'

'Okay, but let me tease him a bit.'

The buzzer sounded and Ice lifted the intercom. 'Hello,' she said in her sexiest voice.

'Ice?' Danny sounded hesitant. 'This is Danny, Jazz's friend.'

'C'mon up, honey. First floor.'

Ice loosened the front of her silk dressing-gown until she had almost revealed her full cleavage. She opened the door as Danny was about to knock and he half-stumbled over the threshold.

'Did you enjoy your trip?' Ice laughed.

'Yeah,' Danny said, irritated, 'but the company was lousy.'

'Oh, we have a smart one here, Jazz,' cooed Ice.

'I need to be, especially around you Noo Yawkers.'

Jazz and Ice laughed. 'This is Danny,' Jazz said.

'Pleased to meet you.'

'Likewise,' said Danny, running his gaze over her. She was tall and Hollywood-beautiful, with a fabulous figure and long blond hair that tumbled artfully down over one shoulder.

'Well, I better go get changed. I'm late already,' said Ice, disappearing into the bedroom. Danny stood gazing after her.

'So, are you going to keep them in your hands all night?' Jazz asked.

Danny looked down at the guitar and bag still hanging from his hands. He smiled sheepishly. 'You got me. Any chance of a cup of tea?'

'Sure.'

As Jazz made the tea, Danny got a chance to look around. The apartment was super-tacky. Pink walls with the carpet a lighter shade of pink. A red leather couch and armchair, both covered with heart-shaped satin cushions, sat at one end of the room, with a smoked glass and chrome coffee table in front of them.

'What do you think?' Jazz asked.

'Nice,' Danny said carefully. 'Yeah, nice.'

Ice came bustling back from the bedroom, wearing a slinky black dress which was open all the way up the back. She turned her back to Danny. 'Do me up, honey.'

'That's what men are for,' Danny said, sighing.

But he smiled as he zipped her up. She plunged back into the bedroom and re-emerged with a thick fur coat over one arm and a soft white leather suitcase in her other hand.

'Okay. That's it, I'm off,' she said. 'You know where everything is, Jazz?'

'Yeah.'

'Okay, kids.' She stopped at the door and looked at Danny. 'You pay for any broken bed springs,' she said with a big wink and then she turned and walked out pulling the door closed behind her.

As soon as she was gone Danny turned to Jazz. 'A complete whirlwind,' he laughed.

'Not as big a whirlwind as this,' Jazz said. She grabbed Danny and pulled him down on to the leather couch. 'She didn't say anything about breaking the couch springs.'

'So you got away all right?' Danny asked, after the couch springs had been thoroughly tested.

Jazz rearranged herself into a sitting position. 'Yeah. I jumped into a taxi on Eighth Street.'

'Your IAD pals went running down Broadway looking for you. Frank and the winos played a blinder as decoys.' He laughed as he pictured the two guys running backwards and forwards frantically on the edge of the crowd.

Jazz laughed too. 'How much did you give him?'

'Ten dollars. And cheap at the price.'

'You're nuts, Irish.' She looked at him, affection obvious in her eyes. 'Did you make any money at the busking?'

'Five dollars and fifty cents and I paid for two cab rides. And that's not counting the ten spot I gave Frank.'

'Not bad, but not exactly a fortune.'

There was a pause that lengthened into an awkward silence.

'Can I ask a question?' Danny asked.

Jazz groaned. 'Don't say it.'

'A cop and a stripper?'

'I knew it.' Jazz jumped up in exasperation and flailed her arms about. 'I knew that's what you were going to ask. Men!'

She flounced around him angrily. 'Well, it's simple. The two of us worked as waitresses a couple of years ago in this café down in SoHo. Ice wanted to be an actress – still does – and I wasn't sure what I wanted to be. She got a job as a dancer and then she was offered more money to strip. She's a good dancer so she gets plenty of tips and now she has a sugar daddy as well and he brings her off to Palm Beach and places.'

'And you became a cop?'

'Yeah. I became a cop.' She nodded as if to underline what she had said.

'But why?'

'I decided to be a cop because I wanted to be a cop.' She could no longer disguise the irritation in her voice.

'Don't get mad,' Danny said. 'I'm just curious.'

'So why are you so curious?' she asked belligerently.

'I don't know, really,' Danny said. 'Maybe it's just that since I met you, you've changed. You seem less like the tough cop. Like in the beginning you were cocky and in total control and then that business with the IAD seemed to rattle you. And I suppose, that business with Vinny, and you letting him knock you around.'

'Jesus, Danny! It wasn't a matter of letting him.' Slowly she began to sob.

'I'm sorry,' said Danny apologetically. He reached up to her. 'Come on. Sit down here beside me.'

She sat down close to him on the couch. He put his arm around her and let her cry gently on his shoulder. They sat in silence until Danny was happy she had recovered.

'Beneath that armadillo skin, Jazz, you're just a big softie like the rest of us, aren't you?'

'S'pose so,' she sniffed. She turned to him, 'Look, Danny, I should've told you from the start, but I had no idea how heavy this was all going to get.'

Danny's heart sank. Told him what? he wondered.

Jazz looked uncomfortable. 'I didn't tell you the real reason I became a cop,' she whispered. 'My brother was a cop,' she blurted out in a rush. 'He's dead now, because that bastard McNally walked him into an ambush.'

'McNally! Jesus!' Danny said angrily.

Jazz began to cry again. This time tears of anger and sorrow combined. 'I'm sorry, Danny, I should've told you before now. I still feel so bad about my brother, that's why I was so anxious to bust that scumbag.'

Danny was taken aback at this sudden revelation. He remained silent for a few minutes and she could see the doubt in his eyes. Did he think that she had used him as a pawn in her game? She took his hand silently.

At last he spoke. 'Fuck me, Jazz, but you're never short on surprises.'

'I swear I wouldn't have kept it from you – except that I thought you had enough shit going on in your head.'

'Mother Teresa, I presume,' he said sarcastically.

'Do you forgive me?' Her expression was anxious.

She saw a tiny smile tickle the corners of his mouth. 'Do I have any option?' he asked. She heaved a sigh of relief. It was going to be all right.

She stood up and took him by the hand. 'Do you want to see the bedroom?'

It reminded Danny of the kind of rooms that saloon madams had in western movies. A kingsize bed and a dressing table took up most of the room. The bed had a crimson velvet cover and once again the walls were pink. A mirror-fronted closet took up almost all of one wall and through its open door, Danny could see a collection of shimmering sequinned dresses.

On the floor in front of the dressing table he spotted a large box of wigs. 'Now that's what I need. A good disguise,' he said, kneeling down and rooting through the box.

'I could use one too,' said Jazz. 'Who would you like? Tina Turner?' She pulled on a Tina Turner wig, looked at herself in the mirror and the two of them howled with laughter.

'Maybe I should try a dress to go with it.'

She rummaged in the closet and pulled out a short silver number. She turned her back on Danny, threw off her jacket and top and slipped the dress over her bare shoulders.

'What do you think?' she asked, turning for approval.

'Groovy,' Danny said. 'Try another one.'

She tried several wigs until she found a red one that suited her face and complexion. She reached into the closet and took out a black dress and slipped it on. It hung low on her breasts and two small straps were all that held it up. She looked at Danny and ran her tongue along her top lip slowly.

'Do you like me, big boy?' she asked, letting the straps slide down off her shoulder to reveal her breasts.

'Jesus, you're beautiful,' Danny said, his voice catching in his throat.

They moved towards one another and as they met in a fierce kiss, sank slowly on to the red velvet cover.

CHAPTER 20

The phone rang. It took Danny a few seconds to uncover it from beneath the heaps of discarded clothes on the floor. It was Jack, he was on his way.

'Shit!' said Danny, covering Jazz's bare shoulder with butterfly kisses. 'I'd forgotten he was coming round to take you to Vinny's. He says he'll be here in about ten minutes. Are you sure you called Vinny?'

'Sure, I'm sure.'

'Okay, just checking.' Danny jumped from the bed and pulled on his clothes. Jazz disappeared into the marble and gold ensuite bathroom for a quick shower. She re-emerged minutes later fully dressed and drying her hair with a towel.

'You're not nervous, are you?'

'A bit,' she confessed.

'If you want me to I'll go with you. Or Jack can go up with you.'

'Danny, trust me. I know Vinny. Let me do it my way.'

The buzzer sounded and Danny opened the door.

Jack wandered in, his jaw dropping in amazement as he took in the decor. Jazz obviously had some interesting friends. But Jack didn't want to waste time chatting. He wanted to get to the bar early – the night before St Patrick's Day was always busy. 'Are you nearly ready, Jazz?' he asked.

'Give me a minute,' she replied.

'How come you were in the neighbourhood, Jack?' Danny asked.

Jack took a deep breath. He would have to sound convincing if he wanted to preserve his cover. It was best if Danny and Jazz didn't know the full truth about him. 'Deirdre told me two fellas came into the bar this morning. I think they were from Immigration so I did a runner from my apartment, and I'm hiding out for a few days in case I lead them to you.'

Danny wanted to know where he was hiding. 'At Eamonn Doherty's place.'

'Eamonn's?' Danny cocked an eyebrow. 'I thought you barely knew him.'

'Aye, that's true,' Jack gulped. 'But after the madness in The Buzz the other night I rang him – just to see if everything was okay – and it turned out we knew loads of people in common. You know us Belfast boys. I even knew a couple of his brothers, so he came down to the bar and we had a few beers.'

'Can we go?' said Jazz, impatiently. She'd hardly listened to their talk in her nervousness.

Danny smiled and gave her a peck on the cheek. 'Good luck.'

Jack drove Jazz across town to Vinny's apartment. They sat outside for a moment while Jazz built up her courage.

'If you want me to go in, I will. And if not, I'll be right outside if you need me,' Jack reassured her.

She leant over and gave him a peck on the cheek. 'Thanks, Jack,' she said, climbing from the car. She walked up the steps, her heart in her mouth, fear gnawing at her stomach. Maybe Danny was right? Maybe she had gone soft over the past few days? She turned and Jack waved comfortingly.

Jazz pushed her sunglasses back firmly on her nose and pressed Vinny's bell. 'It's Jazz,' she said into the intercom.

'C'mon up,' she heard him say.

She climbed the two flights of stairs to his apartment, wetting her lips nervously. She wasn't relishing the encounter.

The door to the apartment was ajar. Jazz knocked.

'I'm in here!' he called.

She walked through the hall and into the lounge. Vinny was sitting on the couch in sweatpants and T-shirt, a can of beer in his hand, his feet resting on the coffee table. The television was tuned to football.

He let her stand for a moment without taking his eyes from the television. When he finally looked up at her, she could see the familiar arrogance in his gaze. 'So how're you doing?' he drawled.

'I'm doing all right.'

'Good. It's nice to see you.' But his smile was cold.

'You needn't disturb your football,' Jazz said. 'It'll only take me a couple of minutes to get my things.'

'Sure thing,' he said. 'Be my guest.'

She went through to the bedroom. With shaking hands she pulled down her two large suitcases. She opened them and, laying them flat on the bed, she began disgorging the contents of drawers into them, cramming the clothes in haphazardly. She just wanted to get out of the place as fast as she could.

'I don't want you to go.' She turned. Vinny was leaning against the door jamb.

'But *I* want to,' Jazz said.

'Listen, we should talk this over. I mean, there's no reason for you to leave. I know I cuffed you 'round a little bit, but it was the first time.'

Jazz turned on him. Pulling off her dark glasses, she pointed to her black eye. 'Is this what you call cuffing me 'round a little bit? Would you like to see some of the other bruises?'

'You made me mad.'

So it was her fault, was it?

'I was tired,' he continued. Still she didn't respond. 'Hey, I'm sorry. And it won't happen again. C'mon.' He moved towards her.

'Don't come near me, Vinny,' she muttered.

'Don't be stupid, Jazz. We're good together.'

'I'm only stupid for not getting out of here sooner. You don't give a shit about me, Vinny, so don't pretend otherwise. I'm just someone to bang when you come in off the road.' She could feel the tears begin to gather at the back of her eyes. She wouldn't soften.

'What are you are you saying? C'mere ...' He moved towards her again.

'Don't, Vinny,' she warned.

'Don't what?'

'I said, don't come near me.'

'Oh yeah?' he said threateningly. He took a step closer.

Jazz reached into her jacket and pulled out her regulation 9mm Beretta. 'Don't come any closer, Vinny.'

He stopped in his tracks. 'For Chrissakes, one fucking black eye and you're going to shoot me?'

'If I have to.' Jazz gripped the gun with both hands to stop the shakes.

His face turned ugly. 'It's that fucking harp who's putting you up to this, isn't it? That fucking Danny guy.'

'Nobody's putting me up to anything. It's my life and my decision. Now back off.'

Jazz snapped the two cases shut with one hand, keeping the gun trained on Vinny with the other.

'Pick up the cases,' she instructed him. She was amazed to hear her voice so firm and strong.

'You think you're going to turn me into your fucking valet as well! No way.'

'Pick up the cases.'

The steel in Jazz's voice convinced Vinny. He took hold of the cases. Jazz backed out the door ahead of him and motioned him to follow. She backed all the way out of the apartment and down the stairs until she was just inside the security door. She fumbled behind her and opened it.

'Is this where you shoot me?' Vinny mocked.

'Go back up the stairs,' Jazz said firmly.

'I should call a cop,' Vinny snarled.

'Go,' Jazz spat.

He backed off and retreated up the stairs, seething with impotence. 'You're fucking nuts. A fucking psycho – that's what you are,' he shouted.

She waited until he had turned the bend in the stairs and then she opened the door quickly and dragged the two cases out. Jack was at her side in an instant and helped her to the car.

As he pulled away from the kerb he turned to her. 'Any trouble?'

'No trouble,' she said, with a smile of satisfaction. 'No trouble at all.'

Jack dropped Jazz and her cases back to Ice's and sped off to My Wild Irish Rose.

'Thanks, Jack,' Jazz called after him in a heartfelt tone. She opened the door and dragged her bags into the apartment. Danny could see that her eyes were ablaze and she was wearing a pleased smile.

'What's the shit-eating grin all about?' he said.

'I did it, Danny.'

'Did what?'

'I did it with Vinny!' In an excited tone she told him what had happened, the words tumbling out in a breathless rush.

Danny listened, the smile on his face growing wider as the story unfolded. 'What did he do?'

'His eyes nearly popped out of his head,' gloated Jazz. 'And, of course, he tried to blame you.'

Danny shrugged. 'I guess it's poor ol' Danny's week for getting blamed for everything in New York.'

'Do you know what I'd love now?' Jazz asked. Danny shook his head.

'A cup of tea.'

Danny threw his eyes to heaven and stretched his arms out in front of him. 'Jesus, we have a convert.'

They both laughed. 'I'll make you a cup of tea, but promise me one thing.'

'What?'

'You'll never pull your gun on me.'

'Only if you refuse to make love to me. Now move, boy.'

CHAPTER 21

Blood spurted from the small nick above Danny's upper lip. He cursed his unsteady hand and the razor in it and watched as the rivulet ran down on to his lips, forcing him to taste its bitterness. Blood attracted and repelled him simultaneously.

He pressed his finger hard against the cut. St Paddy's Day. He wasn't sure if it was his hangover or fear that was making his hand shake. The thought of doing a runner now was tempting. But then he'd never know what might come of his meeting with King Records. And those Immigration guys would never let him into the States again – that'd be his chance of a Green Card scuppered.

Well, St Patrick, it's your big day that I'm sticking round for, he thought. Maybe you could pull some strings for me?

He heard a knock on the door. He wiped his face with a towel as he walked from the bathroom, each step in perfect synchronicity with a stabbing pain in his head.

'Who is it?' he called out.

'It's the St Patrick fairy.' Unmistakably Jazz. Jesus, he hadn't even heard her go out.

He opened the door. She stood there with a large smile on her face. On her head she had a plastic green derby and on her lapel was a large button with 'How Would You Like To Have Irish Relations – With Me!'

'Happy St Paddy's Day,' she said, proffering a bottle of champagne, a carton of orange juice and a similar green hat for Danny.

He kissed her gently. 'Thank you, good fairy. How did you know that Buck's Fizz was St Patrick's favourite tipple?'

She followed him in and closed the door. 'Was it really his favourite drink?' She looked at his solemn face. 'You're kidding me again, aren't you?'

'I guess so,' Danny laughed. Then he groaned, 'It even hurts when I laugh.'

'I'm not surprised,' said Jazz. 'You were shitfaced last night.'

'Well, we had to celebrate old Vinny getting ticked off, didn't we? I hope I wasn't too boisterous,' Danny said contritely.

'A bit,' she scolded. 'But I forgave you.'

'Did we ...?' He smiled and raised an eyebrow.

'No. You were a gentleman and you tried, but that's about it.'

Danny opened the champagne with a loud pop. He held up his glass and toasted her. '*Go mbeirimid beo ar an am seo arís*. That's an old Irish toast,' he explained. 'It means, may we be alive this time next year.'

'No problem.' She grinned.

'I hope you're right. But just in case, don't you think we ought to ...'

'... take up where we left off last night?'

'Well, yeah,' Danny said.

'Irish,' she said, 'that's what I like about you. You're never going to let a little something like a hangover or a matter of life and death come before sex.'

Outside, the day was fighting hard to be warm. A brittle sun was doing its best to claw its way through the smog, but the large crowds lining Fifth Avenue were well buttoned-up to watch the St Patrick's Day parade.

Danny and Jazz stood for a while and watched the bands march past. They would have to cross Fifth Avenue on foot before they could hail a cab for My Wild Irish Rose. The only other alternative was to take a cab to the Village and circumnavigate the parade. Dressed as they were, with Danny head-to-toe in green, and Jazz in a fiery red wig, they could easily be mistaken for participants.

'I think we should eat something before we go to the bar,' said Danny. 'Once we're in there we'll be trapped and we probably won't get anything to eat for the rest of the day.'

Jazz spotted a restaurant a few doors down the block, and dragged him through the doorway.

The restaurant was dowdy and eerily quiet inside. They sat down at a table covered in an ageing oilskin cloth. A lumpy waitress in a faded apron put two glasses of water and two menus on their table.

Danny looked at the menu and snorted. 'What are you doing to me, Jazz? My national feast day and you have me eating in a Polish restaurant!'

She shrugged. 'So what did St Patrick do anyway that was so great that half New York comes to a halt for him?'

'He banished the snakes from Ireland – and they all came to America and became cops and politicians and ever since the parade is a way of thanking him for creating so much employment.'

'Very funny, mister,' she smiled. 'Do you have a parade in Dublin?'

'Yeah, but it's Mickey Mouse compared to this one. It lasts about an hour or two but the kids love it.'

They both reacted sharply to the mention of Danny's kids.

'Do you miss them?' Jazz asked. The question sounded hollow to her own ears and she wasn't sure if she wanted to hear the answer.

''Course I do.' Danny didn't say anything for a while, just stared at the table. Then he raised his eyes. 'Yeah, I do, a lot. 'Specially in the mornings.'

'You must be looking forward to seeing them?'

'Yeah. I am. Except I rang Mary yesterday and she froze me out.'

'Well, maybe it'll be different when you're home.'

He locked on to her eyes and wouldn't let her turn away. 'I'm definitely on my way out of here, aren't I?' he said.

'Yes,' she said quietly, returning his stare. Whatever happened to McNally, Immigration would make sure that Danny was sent packing. It was just a matter of time. Her eyes filled. 'I'm sorry, Danny. I know I'm just being stupid. I just got more attached to you than I should have.'

He reached across the ugly oilcloth and held her hand. 'I'm pretty attached to you too,' he said softly. 'It's all such a bummer. I get a good gig, I get good vibes from a record company and what happens?' His voice rose in mock anger. 'Here I am on St Patrick's Day, hungover, sitting in a Polish restaurant with a cop who feeds me champagne and good sex and instead of being able to take her off and fill her full of green beer and *more* sex, I have to go and put my ass on the line to bust some bent cop. Is there no justice for the Irish on this day-of-days?'

Jazz laughed and wiped at her tears. 'Irish, you cheer me up. I wish you were staying.'

CHAPTER 22

Black 47's 'Funky Ceili' was blasting out of the jukebox in the window of My Wild Irish Rose, washing over the crowd that was growing bigger by the minute. A frisson of expectation and excitement was jumping from person to person, like a streak of lightning run wild.

Jack drank it all in. He was glad he had trusted his instincts and arrived early again. It had given him a chance to make up his Simple Syrup and his Margarita mixes. It was going to be a busy one, and himself, Deirdre, and Con, the extra bartender, would be stretched to the limit to keep up with demand for drinks.

He scanned the crowd again. His street radar was on full alert for anyone who looked even a little bit out of place. He had designated the stretch inside the door as his station on the bar. From there he could see the new arrivals, as well as keep an eye on those already inside. Under the counter, his gun was concealed in a box beneath a sheaf of papers.

He felt a tingle in his body, a wild energy that seemed to reach into every fibre in his system, a sensation of readiness he hadn't felt since his days on the streets of Belfast. Oddly enough, he felt no fear. If the Immigration guys arrived, he would make a run for it. If McNally arrived and he had to take action, he was ready for that too. Most of all he felt relief, a release from the limbo of his phoney identity.

Jazz waited as Danny paid off the cab half a block from My Wild Irish Rose. He turned to her. 'Walk on there ahead of me a bit. I want to have a quick toke and I don't want you busted, though God knows in that wig, even your own mother wouldn't recognise you.'

'Are you sure you should smoke, Danny? You need to be on your toes,' Jazz said anxiously.

'I'll have you know, my good woman, when I smoke I become Rudolf Nureyev.'

'Yeah? Well, he's dead.'

'Very funny. Very Woody Allen. Go on there and let the man smoke his joint.'

Jazz walked ahead of him a few paces and watched over her shoulder as Danny sucked in the smoke. He flicked the top off the joint after a few big drags and joined her again. 'That's better. Get me in the mood.'

'Whatever happened to old-fashioned drink?' Jazz asked sardonically.

'I intend to do my share of that as well, but only when I'm sure McNally and Lee Harvey Oswald are not in the bar.'

'Who's Woody Allen now? Are you not even a little bit afraid?'

'No, ma'am, I'm a big bit afraid. But I worked it out. All over the world there are guys who would slit their mother's throat to be playing in New York tonight and I'm actually doing it. And if things work out my whole life could soon be changed forever.'

'Or it could be over.'

'Does that mean you think I should abandon my dream and go home and get a job in my dad's friend's factory? For shame, woman. You have a wicked streak of pessimism in you. Get in that door.'

Jack saw the bar door open. Danny came in and fought his way towards him, a big grin on his face as he saw the size of the crowd. Behind him came a very pretty redhead who Jack didn't recognise. When Danny put his arm around her Jack looked again more closely and saw that it was Jazz.

'Jesus, you nearly fooled me, Jazz,' he exclaimed. 'Brilliant wig. Hey, Danny! Happy St Patrick's Day.'

They ordered their usual – a Flag and a Rolling Rock. Then Danny turned to Jazz. 'Anyone you recognise?'

'Nah. Nobody that looks like my two pet assholes.' She positioned herself at the other end of the bar from Jack so she'd have a clear view of the crowd.

'Just because you nearly shot old Vinny Boy doesn't mean you have to turn into Rambette permanently,' teased Danny.

'No. But I bet you're happier that someone carrying a gun is looking after you.'

Danny didn't like to admit it, but it was true.

'While we're on about it, gorgeous,' he said, 'what do I do if your two stooges come in?'

'You do nothing. They mightn't recognise me and they won't make a move unless McNally comes in. You're the bait, remember?'

'And what about the Immigration boys?'

'It looks like they're making a special exception for you and McNally and are helping each other. I'd say they're looking for one big bust when they pull in you and McNally.'

'A kind of assholes stick-together-thing?' Danny asked.

'Get up and sing, fool,' said Jazz, laughing. 'And don't forget to sing one for me.'

CHAPTER 23

Danny left Jazz at the bar and pushed his way to the stage where he turned on the amplifier and checked his guitar tuning. He could feel the butterflies in his stomach but the dope had taken the edge off his fear.

The bar was really packed and the heat was already starting to show in beads of sweat on foreheads. Danny loved this atmosphere more than anything else. This was his thrill, an audience waiting to be impressed.

What a madhouse, he thought. The crowd was like a fire all ready to light. All he had to do was come up with the match. He decided to try something really thicko like 'McNamara's Band'. This crowd was bound to treat it like it was superhip.

Oh, me name is McNamara ...

Wasn't I right? he congratulated himself. Hardly one line into the song and they're in a frenzy.

> Oh, the drums go bang and the cymbals clang and
> the horns ...

I don't know what I'm so happy about. This kind of mayhem is great cover for those bastards from the Immigration and the IAD – and McNally. The thought washed over him like a bucket of cold water.

> A credit to old Ireland is McNamara's Band.

'Thank you, thank you, thank you, for your generous applause. For a bunch of rowdies, you've got remarkably good taste. This time,' he said, looking down at Jazz, 'I'm going to rock it up for someone a bit special.'

Jazz smiled up at him and acknowledged Danny's dedication with a wink. Danny was quite a showman and she noticed how the women were responding to him.

'Anybody suspicious?' Jack's voice startled her.

'No,' she said jumpily. Jesus, she'd forgotten completely that she was supposed to be on the alert, not watching Danny's show.

'Sorry, Jazz, I gave you a start. So, nobody yet?' Jack had abandoned his station at the other end of the bar to check in.

'Nah. Not so far anyway, and I'll be real happy if I don't all night.' She paused. 'Jack, answer me something?'

'Go ahead.'

'If the Immigration guys bust Danny, will they lock him up straight off?' She could have checked it out at the precinct house, but she was worried about raising anyone's suspicions.

Jack froze for a moment. Did Jazz know anything about him or was she just asking an innocent question? 'I don't know anything about that procedure,' he lied.

'There's a back way out of here, isn't there?' Jazz said.

'Yeah.' Jack pointed to the way he had taken the day before. 'Out through the kitchen. It leads out to the lane at the back and that runs all the way between Twenty-seventh and Twenty-eighth.'

'Okay. Thanks. It's good to know – just in case.'

'Well, that's it, boys and girls, ladies and gentlemen,' Danny was roaring into the microphone. 'I'm taking a little break now to review my act and if I don't come back you'll know I've broken up,' he joked. 'But I think seeing as it's the day that's in it, I'll hang in there.'

Danny pulled his guitar off and dimmed the spotlight on the stage. 'Fuck me, it's warm,' he whispered to himself.

He made his way through a forest of punters, stopping for words of congratulations or requests for songs. Finally he reached Jazz.

'They love you,' she said.

'Class will out.' Danny smiled. 'I need to get a breath of fresh air. Will you hold on here?'

'Yeah, sure,' she said sounding a little hurt, 'if you want to be on your own.'

'It's not a question of wanting to be on my own, Jazz. It's just that I won't be long. I'm going to have another quick lash of my joint.'

She smiled and nodded.

Danny pulled the door open and the cold blast of night air smacked him in the face. An overflow crowd spilled on to the pavement. He leaned back against the window and sipped on his drink.

'Are you Danny?'

Danny raised his head to see who had asked the question. He saw a good-looking man in an expensive suit, about his own height and age, but with very dark hair and a sallow complexion. He looked coiled and ready to spring. A cold hand closed around Danny's heart.

Is this him? he thought. McNally's hit man? Is this where it's all going to end? Oh Jesus, where's Jazz?

'Who wants to know?' Danny asked nervously, drawing himself up to a standing position.

'I do,' the dark man said. 'You fucked me up with Jazz.' He pushed closer, his eyes blazing with temper.

'Vinny!' Danny exclaimed. 'You're Vinny, aren't you?'

'Yeah, I'm Vinny.'

Danny, emboldened now that he knew this was not one of McNally's thugs, reacted aggressively. 'You fucked yourself up with Jazz, mate.'

'And I say you did it,' Vinny spat out through clenched teeth. He pushed Danny back against the window with the heel of his hand.

'Watch it, pal,' said Danny, jerking the hand away. Vinny looped a punch at him. It caught Danny high on the temple. He took the blow and made an awkward attacking lunge. Vinny neatly side-stepped and using Danny's momentum against him, threw him to the ground.

The crowd scattered as Vinny aimed a kick at Danny's head. His foot never reached its destination. Jack, hurtling out of nowhere, took Vinny in a flying tackle and pinned him to the ground.

'Don't fucking move,' Jack said, pressing his gun to Vinny's temple.

Vinny whimpered.

'Hold it, Jack! Hold it!' Jazz was down beside him. 'Don't do nothing. That's Vinny.'

'Vinny!' Jack said disbelievingly.

Danny was back on his feet. 'Let me at him!'

Jazz stood up in front of Danny. 'Keep cool!' she hissed through her teeth. 'Don't make this any bigger than it is now.'

'What the fuck is this, Jazz?' Vinny shouted. Jack still had him pinned to the ground. 'This guy's got a goddamn gun!'

'Let him go, Jack,' Jazz ordered.

Jack released his grip on Vinny who got up and started to smooth down his suit. He was cursing under his breath.

'Jack, what the –' Danny said, suddenly seeing the gun in Jack's hand.

'I said cool it,' Jazz hissed again. 'Jack, get rid of the gun, now.'

Jack responded immediately. He walked quickly back into the pub and was swallowed up in the crowd.

Jazz spoke to the people who had scattered to the fringes of the sidewalk. 'Okay, everybody, I'm a cop and it's all over. Just go back inside now.' She turned to Danny. 'Inside. Now! Go!'

'What about him?' Danny pointed at Vinny.

She looked at Vinny with unconcealed disdain. 'Don't worry. I can take care of him.'

Jack felt the adrenalin whizzing through his bloodstream. He should be scared of the madness that overrode all his commonsense, but when he had spotted the commotion through the window, he hadn't hesitated for as much as a second. A force inside, or outside himself, had galvanised him into instant action. He had grabbed his gun and jumped the counter. He was outside the door before he could stop himself.

He had scarcely realised his gun was at Vinny's head until he heard Jazz's voice. If she hadn't stopped him would he have pulled the trigger? He couldn't answer his own question. It all seemed like some surreal flashback.

If he got out of this jam, he decided, he would throw his gun into the East River and head for San Francisco and start all over again. This time he would be in control of his life. This time he would 'live' not just do time.

Through the throng of drinkers, he saw Danny and Jazz jabbering animatedly at one another. With a bit of Irish luck, everything would work out.

On the other side of the bar Jazz and Danny were still arguing. Jazz put her hand on Danny's arm and stared into his eyes. She hoped he would believe her. 'Danny, I told you already, I swear Vinny was the last person I expected to show up tonight.'

'I suppose you were flattered that he was upset enough to bother,' Danny said bitterly.

'That kind of shit is unnecessary, Danny. I know Vinny better than you and he didn't show up for me. He showed up for himself, because he couldn't bear to think that somebody would get the better of him.'

'Yeah, well he got the better of me,' Danny said ruefully. He hated to think of being face down on the sidewalk in front of all those people. In front of Jazz in particular.

'Physically, Danny. That's all. He didn't get the better of you any other way and that counts for more than sticking a punch on somebody.'

'Well, I didn't need that on top of everything else.'

Jazz stroked his hair soothingly. 'Cool it.'

'How the fuck can I?' Vinny's attack had suddenly made the danger real.

'Here, I'll get you another drink,' Jazz offered.

'You'd better send it up to me while I'm singing. If I don't start again soon, this mob, as well as everybody else, will be after my blood.'

She watched him fight his way to the mike and his guitar. Should she stop him now and forget about McNally? Before she got a chance to make up her mind, Danny flicked on the spotlight and started to sing.

CHAPTER 24

Danny couldn't believe the response of the crowd. There was nothing in his experience to compare to it. In the seven years he had been singing, he had never been short of appreciation, but this was extravagant beyond belief. The punters were standing shoulder to shoulder in front of him and all the way to the back of the pub. Those who had chairs were standing on them. More were standing on tables and five girls were dancing on the countertop between the bar and the seating area.

Outside the window, a crowd five-deep was dancing to the music, waving at him, their faces pressed up against the glass.

He was giving them all the old favourites.

No nay, never, no more
Will I play the wild rover
No never, no more ...

Danny found himself grinning inanely. Somehow people were making space to dance. He searched the crowd for Jazz, but she had disappeared

Panic struck. Jesus, Jazz, don't go missing on me, he pleaded silently. Where are you?

He scanned the faces frantically. Where was Jack? And where had he got that gun?

Danny heard loud knocking on the window behind him. He turned and saw Jazz outside. She had pushed a piece of paper flat against the glass. Danny leaned over and read it.

```
McNally just left The Buzz.
Here soon.
Stay cool.
I'll watch for him.
```

Danny acknowledged the note with a nod. His stomach lurched. He looked across at the bar and could just about see Jack shoving a clenched fist in the air to him as a sign of solidarity. He leaned into the microphone. 'Yo, Jack. Happy trails.' His voice sounded thin and distant.

'Sing "Danny Boy",' a voiced called out from the crowd.

'Yeah, "Danny Boy",' a second voice called. A chant began, '"Danny Boy". Sing "Danny Boy". Sing "Danny Boy".'

'Okay, okay,' Danny said over the microphone. 'Seems only right as my name is Danny. The least I can do is sing my own song. But I want you all to help.'

> Oh Danny Boy,
> The pipes the pipes are calling
> From glen to glen
> And down the mountain side ...

The pub suddenly came to order. The crowd, as one, were singing the song with the reverence of a hymn, their faces solemn, their voices soft and even tuneful, the notes soaring and swooping through the smoky haze, drinks forgotten as the melody swept them along on a wave of unabashed sentimentality.

> But come ye back
> When summer's in the meadow
> Or when the valley's hushed and white with snow
> 'Tis I'll be *here* –

Danny turned his head as he hit the highest note in the song. In that instant he glimpsed from the corner of his eye a burly figure approaching the side window, his arms stretched out in front of him in a shooting position. Danny ducked instinctively just as he saw the flash from McNally's gun. The window shattered, sending glass flying in all directions. Something whipped into Danny's shoulder with a hot searing pain and the force spun him into the front row of the audience.

The crowd melted back from the stage, screaming in fright and pain from wounds caused by flying glass. Jack, gun in hand, fought his way through. As he jumped on stage he fired at McNally who stood outside the window, surveying his work. A bullet ripped into him. McNally staggered back, recovered his balance and then fired again. Jack crumpled to the floor.

Jazz jumped over Danny on the floor. Another shot rang out and Danny saw McNally, his face contorted in rage, keel over and fall in slow motion out of his line of vision.

'Danny! Danny! Are you all right?' Jazz was at his side, cradling him in her arms.

He looked up at her. 'It's my shoulder. Jack? I think he's in a bad way. Help me up.'

She lifted Danny up and helped him to where Jack lay on the stage. Danny turned him over gently with his uninjured arm. A thin trickle of blood ran from the corner of his mouth. He looked at them and smiled wanly.

'Live by the gun, die by the gun,' he murmured softly.

'You won't die,' Danny said frantically. Jazz squeezed Danny's arm to try and calm him. He turned and shouted towards the bar. 'Get an ambulance! Somebody get an ambulance!' He looked down again. Jack's head had slumped on his arm.

'Ah Jesus, Jesus, Jesus!' Danny cried. 'No, Jack! No!'

Suddenly the bar was full of cops. Danny looked at them, tears streaming down his cheeks. 'Where the fuck were you a few moments ago!' he yelled, his anguish turning his voice into a wail. He spotted the two guys from IAD. 'Are you happy now? Was this the only way your lousy plan could work?'

Jazz helped him to his feet and walked him to the bar. People were standing frozen in disbelief, not quite sure of what they had seen.

'We'd better get you to a hospital, hon,' she said.

'In a minute,' Danny said. Jazz put her arm around him. He shivered and began to cry again. 'Jack, the poor fucker.' She leaned over and took Jack's jacket from behind the counter and draped it around Danny's shoulders.

Outside disoriented customers milled about on the sidewalk as two more police cars screeched into the kerb, sirens blaring, blue lights flashing. Close behind came an ambulance.

A young policeman approached them at the counter. 'Ma'am, the ambulance is ready now. If you'd like to come with him that's fine.'

She turned to Danny. 'Would you like me to come with you?'

'You'd better stay and clear up all the shit here. Try and keep it as clean as possible, if you know what I mean.'

'Excuse me, Mr Toner.' Danny looked up to see two men in suits. 'I'm John O'Brien and this is Tony di Mucci from Immigration. Just to let you know we'll be coming to talk to you at the hospital when they've fixed you up.' Danny just looked at them, his mouth fixed in a grim line.

'I'll come in and see you later,' Jazz said. She kissed him on the cheek.

Danny followed the young cop to the ambulance with the jacket still draped around his shoulders. He held his wound with his good hand. The pain was throbbing now in all its fury and he felt nauseous.

Jesus, he thought, it could be me lying dead there. What a gobshite I am. What about Mary and the kids? Who'd look after them if I was ...

The ambulance pulled away from the kerb, jogging him out of his thoughts. Its siren blared a stark fugue through a landscape of red and blue flashing lights. Danny looked back through the window at the receding scene. For all the world, he might be looking at the end of a cop show on television – except there was no glib ending, no credits to roll and Jack would not be around to play a part in another episode.

CHAPTER 25

The sun was warm with the welcome of spring as Danny and Jazz emerged from the hospital the next morning. Danny was wearing the same green jeans, but Jazz had bought him a new white shirt. His arm was tightly bound to his chest in a sling and he still had Jack's jacket draped around his shoulders. Nobody had asked for it, and he wasn't going to volunteer it. He looked back at the hospital and tried to remember the detail, so that he could make a record in his head of all the places he had been in his last few hours in New York.

'It's cruel, isn't it?' he said. 'Spring arrives with a vengeance on the very day they kick me out.'

'You mean the day you voluntarily exit,' Jazz corrected him. 'It makes a difference.'

They climbed into the waiting cab and directed the driver. 'Jazz,' Danny said, 'are you the police officer officially in charge of me until I "voluntarily exit"?'

'Sort of,' she replied. 'I promised I'd have you ready in Sixth Street at four-thirty.'

'To hand over to Laurel and Hardy from Immigration.'

'They seem nice enough guys.'

'Yeah, I suppose so. Don't mind me. It's all such a fuck-up, I still can't believe it.' He looked at her and smiled weakly. 'I was starting to like New York too. Out there are millions of people bitching about another Monday in Manhattan and here I am wishing I could swop with any one of them.'

'It's like what you were saying the other night about so many guys envying you singing here,' Jazz reminded him.

'Yep. On the button. And now the canary has been silenced.'

They rode to The Buzz without talking. Maybe he was imagining it, but Danny thought he noticed people on the sidewalks responding to the bright warm sun with a new jauntiness in their steps. Even the traffic seemed less frantic, more orderly. He craned his neck and looked up at the sun glancing off the glass skyscrapers, bathing the city in blinding optimism.

They climbed out of the cab at Seventy-third Street. Eamonn saw them through the window and came out to greet them.

'How are you doing, Danny?' he asked solemnly. 'How's the shoulder?'

'I'm fine thanks, Eamonn. It's sore, but I'll live.'

He led them inside where he had reserved a table by the window. Robbie came over and shook hands with Danny. 'I'm glad you're all right, squire,' he said sincerely.

Danny thanked him.

'If there's anything you need, tell me.'

'I need my head examined.' Danny's joke only lifted the gloom slightly. Robbie disappeared to organise drinks and some food.

'I was going to say this is like The Last Supper,' Danny said. 'The Last Lunch doesn't sound quite as impressive.'

No one laughed. It was too close to the bone.

'I'd have come to see you at the hospital,' put in Eamonn, 'but Jazz said it'd be better if we all stayed as far away as possible – for our own sakes.' It was true, the hospital had been crawling with cops asking questions.

'I understand, Eamonn. Anyway, Supercop here was around to take care of me.'

Jazz smiled and put her arm around him. 'He's a bad patient.'

Eamonn looked at Jazz. 'There was very little in the papers about it. Did somebody put the lid on it?'

'Big time,' she said. 'It suited the cops not to have the story about McNally blow up. The fact that he died suited them even more.'

'And what about Jack?' Eamonn asked.

'They knew who he was,' Danny interjected. 'The two guys from Immigration told me in the hospital. But because the story would be messy politically for everyone, they'd been sitting on it till a policy decision was made. Jack would've been a big catch. They're quite happy to bury the story and poor old Jack along with it.'

But there were other interested parties, as Eamonn knew. 'What about the Provos?'

'Not eager to draw attention to themselves,' Danny shrugged. 'As for me, they reckon I won't go home and blab because I still want a Green Card to get back into America again.'

'You do?' Eamonn said incredulously.

'Sure,' Danny smiled. 'I know it's nuts, but I've developed a taste for New York. I like it.' He held out his injured arm in front of him. 'Even with this, even with Jack dead.'

'Poor bastard,' Eamonn sighed. 'Was it McNally who got him?'

'Yeah. I got hit first, then Jack came flying and shot McNally, but the big ox was able to get off a shot and he hit Jack.'

'And then McNally got shot?'

'Yeah,' Danny continued. 'Jazz here knows more about that than I do.' It all seemed a confused blur now.

Jazz took up the story. 'I saw Jack shoot McNally, but he got back up and managed to shoot Jack. I fired a shot at him and that was it.'

Danny reached into the inside pocket of the jacket and pulled out the photograph of Jack and his four companions. 'Do you know who these fellas are? I found this in Jack's pocket.'

Eamonn took the photograph in both hands. He stared at it for quite a while and then he gave a sad smile. He spoke softly. 'That's my brother, Michael, on the right-hand side of him. The other three lads were also part of the Famous Five, as everybody called them. They're all dead now. Jack was the last to go.'

'I'm sorry, Eamonn,' Danny said. 'I didn't realise what the picture meant. Keep it.'

Eamonn shook his head. 'That's okay. I did my grieving for my brother a long time ago and it's well and truly over.'

'D'you know the last thing Jack said? Live by the gun, die by the gun.'

'How right he was.'

Danny linked his arm with Jazz's. He sniffed the air and then set off walking at a good steady pace.

'Hey, Irish. Where are you going?'

'Would you mind if we got the subway and walked down St Mark's Place?'

'Can you manage it?'

''Course I can. Aren't I a horse of a man?'

'Just don't go fainting on me.'

They walked to the subway. Danny descended the steps and bought three tokens.

'What do you need three for? There's only the two of us.'

'Yeah, well, I'm buying it as part of my New York survival kit,' he said, stuffing the extra one in his pocket.

'A survival kit?'

'Yeah. Don't laugh. I worked it out that everybody who comes to New York should have a survival kit.'

'Oh yeah? And what's in the kit?'

'One subway token, two Alka-Seltzer, a five dollar bill in case you have to get a cab, a strong pair of brogues in case you have to do a lot of walking, two Paracetamol in case you have a hangover, a condom in case you get lucky, a large joint in case you want to get out of it ... and finally, in the event of being really desperate for a place to stay, the phone number of a distant relative who lives in the Bronx.'

Jazz laughed. 'And when are you going to use this?'

'When I come back.'

'So you *are* going to come back.'

'Sure,' he mocked. 'You can't expect a man to stop following his dream that easily.'

'What about your wife and kids? You said you thought she might take you back.'

'I don't know about that yet, Jazz.' The lightness went out of his voice. 'I'll have to work on that when I get home. In the meantime, let's not talk about it.'

They got off the subway at Astor Place and walked up into the sunlight. Danny drank it all in – Broadway, Fourth Avenue, The Public Theatre, St Mark's stretching before him. Eight blocks from home.

They crossed over to St Mark's Place. Danny scrutinised everybody they passed, stopping to look into shops, peering through restaurant windows. Every sign, every flashing light, every bit of graffiti, became a detail on a great canvas.

Danny's mind spun off. Goodbye, Noo Yawk – for the moment, he mused. So long, you cracked pavements, arty-farties, all you hippies, all you mourners in black. I've got to go, just when I was getting the hang of you. I've taken a bullet and lived – that's even flashier than a Green Card.

'Are you there?' Jazz's voice snapped Danny to attention.

'Sorry,' he said. 'I was saying some mental farewells to the streets here. I love walking down here, just for the buzz. I always felt I was part of a great movement of people all running towards some golden light – fame, money, better still a combination of both.'

'Irish,' Jazz said stopping. 'You are the biggest dreamer I ever met.'

'So is there something wrong with that?' he asked turning to face her.

'No. I guess I'm a bit of a dreamer too.'

'Tell me, what are you dreaming about then?' he asked, searching her face for signs.

'Well, I know now that I'm happy being a cop and all. And I think I'll probably transfer to regular duties. With a bit of luck, I might make detective.'

They walked on slowly. 'Big Shot Detective. I like the sound of that. You'll make it too.'

She squeezed his arm. He had a knack of making her feel good.

'Jazz, I never asked you and I should've. I suppose I was too caught up in myself. But how did it feel to shoot someone? Was it weird?'

Jazz had been trying to avoid thinking about it. Now she had to face it. 'Kind of weird afterwards, but at the time it just sort of happened. Like I'm not trying to trivialise it or anything but I just did what had to be done.'

'And it was your bullet that killed McNally for definite?'

'Yeah. It was. Got him in the heart.'

'Sweet revenge?'

She hesitated. 'For my brother? No. It wasn't. At the end of it all, there was no satisfaction. Is that weird or what?'

They said nothing for a while, walking slowly and deliberately across First Avenue.

Then Danny spoke again. 'While we're at it, there's one last question I need to clear up, Officer. What's Jazz short for? Jasmine?'

'Short for nothing,' answered Jazz, looking shy for the first time he could remember. 'My real name is Dolores.'

'*Dolores!*' Danny let the name roll off his tongue and laughed out loud. 'Detective Dolores Ma*hony*. I like it.'

Danny let Jazz carry his bag and guitar and set them down at the apartment door. He took a last look around his bedroom and pulled the door closed. In his hand he held a final note from Gail.

> Some people are careless about where they leave cups and mugs which can be knocked over. Please return all such implements to their proper places after use.

'I'll have to leave her a note myself,' he said. He pulled a pen from his pocket and wrote on the back of Gail's note.

> A mug is not an implement, asshole.
> Happy bean farts

The sudden shrill burst of the buzzer cut through their laughter. 'Well, I guess it's time to go,' said Jazz.

Danny looked at her. She came over and kissed him tenderly. He felt a surge of passion and pressed her body to his. She reached down and started to undo his fly. Before he could stop her, she was on her knees.

He wanted to say stop, but his body was responding. He closed his eyes and stroked her hair gently, letting himself go. Would anything ever be normal again?

A minute later, the buzzer sounded impatiently. Jazz stood up, her eyes glistening.

'Sshh ... remember,' Danny murmured. 'We promised. No tears.'

'No tears.'

Jazz opened the door and picked up his bag.

Danny followed her out carrying his guitar. He did up the three separate locks and slid the keys back in underneath the door. The phone in the apartment began to ring as he started down the stairs.

For a moment Danny hesitated, then over his shoulder he shouted, 'Fuck you, whoever you are!' And he ran down the stairs and out into the sunlight on East Sixth Street.

Inside the apartment, the answering machine clicked on:

> Hi. This is Rick Dawdle from King Records for Danny Toner. Danny, everybody here loves your tape. We want to talk to you. Call me and we'll set up a meeting. Bye.

WITHDRAWN FROM STOCK